D0338049

THROWAWAY
GIRL

CALGARY PUBLIC LIBRARY

NOV 2014

THROWAWAY
GIRL

kristine scarrow

DUNDURN
TORONTO

Copyright © Kristine Scarrow, 2014

All rights reserved. No part of this publication may be reproduced, stored in a retrieval system, or transmitted in any form or by any means, electronic, mechanical, photocopying, recording, or otherwise (except for brief passages for purposes of review) without the prior permission of Dundurn Press. Permission to photocopy should be requested from Access Copyright.

All characters in this work are fictitious. Any resemblance to real persons, living or dead, is purely coincidental.

Editor: Carrie Gleason
Design: Jennifer Gallinger
Cover design by Courtney Horner
Cover image: © Sanjay Deva
Printer: Webcom

Library and Archives Canada Cataloguing in Publication

Scarrow, Kristine, author
    Throwaway girl / Kristine Scarrow.

Issued in print and electronic formats.
ISBN 978-1-4597-1407-6 (pbk.).--ISBN 978-1-4597-1408-3 (pdf)
--ISBN 978-1-4597-1409-0 (epub)

    I. Title.

PS8637.C37T47 2014   jC813'.6   C2013-908363-4   C2013-908364-2

1   2   3   4   5   18   17   16   15   14

 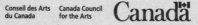

Conseil des Arts du Canada   Canada Council for the Arts

ONTARIO ARTS COUNCIL
CONSEIL DES ARTS DE L'ONTARIO
an Ontario government agency
un organisme du gouvernement de l'Ontario

We acknowledge the support of the **Canada Council for the Arts** and the **Ontario Arts Council** for our publishing program. We also acknowledge the financial support of the **Government of Canada** through the **Canada Book Fund** and **Livres Canada Books**, and the **Government of Ontario** through the **Ontario Book Publishing Tax Credit** and the **Ontario Media Development Corporation**.

Care has been taken to trace the ownership of copyright material used in this book. The author and the publisher welcome any information enabling them to rectify any references or credits in subsequent editions.

J. Kirk Howard, President

The publisher is not responsible for websites or their content unless they are owned by the publisher.

Printed and bound in Canada.

Visit us at
Dundurn.com | *@dundurnpress* | *Facebook.com/dundurnpress* | *Pinterest.com/dundurnpress*

Dundurn
3 Church Street, Suite 500
Toronto, Ontario, Canada
M5E 1M2

To Gracelyn, Ethan, and Kale — may you always believe in your dreams, especially when life doesn't go the way you planned. The future is yours for the taking.

Chapter 1

I haven't always been called Andy. For a good chunk of my life, my name was Bernice, the name my mother gave me. How my mother and I ever got paired up will forever be a mystery to me. I don't know why she kept me in the first place, but she did.

Although she gave birth to me, I refer to my mother by her name, Jacqueline. I don't know who my father is, and perhaps I'll never find out. "It could have been any one of a hundred men," Jacqueline told me as I was growing up. Nothing can instill pride for a mother faster than a line like that, don't you think?

I'm about to turn eighteen. And that means leaving Haywood House, the place I've lived the longest since I was taken away from my mother. A group home may not be a "real" home, the kind most kids grow up in, but for some of us, it might be the only stable home we've ever known.

As far as looks go, I'm pretty average, I guess. I mean, I don't look like Lisa Carson, the popular, albeit stupid, girl here at Haywood, but I have my own sense of style. I'm not into the trendy, girly wear that I see in the stores (not that I can afford it anyway), but I'm not sporting that evil army look, either. Last time I saw a kid wearing that stuff, I nearly dove to the ground for safety when he entered the convenience store. Frankly, as far as fashion goes, I'm about as normal as it gets.

I have straight blonde hair and green eyes. If we're getting technical here, I was born a brunette. Someone said once that blondes have more fun so I decided I needed to be blonde. Then I'd have more fun. Funny thing is … I'm still waiting.

At the moment, Gertie, the night supervisor is coming my way. She's going to tell me it's time for lights out. I look up, and sure enough, she is ambling over to me with that sideways gait she has, like she's had something shoved up her butt and can't get it out. I know this is a mean thing to say, being that Gertie is fairly nice and all, but seriously! Watch her walk and you can't help but comment.

I click off the small lamp on the metal bedside table and bury myself deep into the scratchy wool blanket. Sandpaper would be a luxury compared to this blanket, but I decide to keep my mouth shut. It could be worse. I've had worse.

Gertie peers around and makes her way across the room. I watch as her body casts a shadow against the wall that could be considered both hilarious and terrifying. The Hunchback of Notre Dame meets Penguin Man or something. I stifle a giggle and give Gertie a break. She really is a pretty nice woman.

I shut my eyes and attempt sleep. I am tired, but I have always had difficulty falling asleep. It's no wonder, given my childhood. I hear the soft snores of the girls around me, jealous of their ability to drift off into the land of dreams. My mind wanders instead to my earliest memories of life with Jacqueline.

Chapter 2

1999

It's winter. I am about six years old. I'm wearing my favourite blue dress, my only dress, which is threadbare and frayed in several places. The dress is so tattered and worn that it has a musty smell to it. It hasn't been washed recently and there is a smear of dirt on the front of it. Despite its look and smell, I love how pretty this dress makes me feel. I've even combed my hair. I am a beautiful princess, worthy of love and attention.

The snow is falling, fat wet flakes that cover the streets and cars as I watch for my mom from our apartment window. I am excited and full of hope. I am thrilled that it is snowing. The snow is so clean and brilliant. It makes the outside shimmer and glisten. All the dirt and ugliness on the streets below is hidden. I stick my hands on the frosted windows, scraping layers of ice off with my fingernails in order to get a better view. I long to run outside with my mouth open wide, eager and searching for the crisp, refreshing flakes on my tongue.

The day couldn't be more perfect. I look and feel amazing. When Mommy comes through the door, she will be happy from how beautiful the snow is, so proud of me, so proud of how I look.

I wait and wait. Mommy wasn't here when I woke up this morning, so there is no telling where she is and how long ago she left. I have done everything I can to make her happy. I've picked up the clothes that littered our bedroom floor; I've rinsed and scrubbed the mound of dishes that have piled on the kitchen counter. It was hard to clean them when all the gooey bits of food have been sitting on them for such a long time. Without having soap to help, I used my fingernails to scrape the dried bits as best as I can. Some of the plates were heavy and hard to handle. One even broke, but I've scooped the pieces up and hidden them and Mommy will never know.

She won't believe how clean it looks in here and that I've done all this work. She might walk in, distracted, talking about something, perhaps what a gorgeous day it's turning out to be and then look up in surprise. She might stop in mid-sentence, gaze around in wonder and then rush to me with an appreciative smile and her arms open wide. She'll hug me so tight that I'll feel like I am suffocating from all her love. Perhaps she'll have gone to the grocery store and be carrying a bulging plastic bag. She'll tell me what a good girl I am, how lucky she is to have me and how beautiful I look; how my light shines brighter than any winter wonderland. Then she'll show me the fresh, delicious food she's bought, and make dinner for just the two of us.

My heart swells with the power of my daydream. Mommy will see how hard I'm trying, what a good girl I really am. She'll be so proud that she'll want to stay home and take care of me. She'll want to spend time with me because she'll see that I can help make her happy. I'm willing her to come through the door, just so I can see the smile I'll put on her face.

It's almost lunch time. I can tell by the way my tummy is rumbling. When I first wake up, it's faint and easy to forget about. But by noon, those faint rumblings gather steam and start to roar, like tigers clawing at my stomach. I already know there is nothing to eat here. I've checked and rechecked the cupboards and the fridge many times in case I've missed something. The bottle of ketchup standing alone in the fridge has been the closest thing to a meal for me today. I've squeezed circles of it, making silly shapes onto a plate, rolling my finger in it, painting mini works of art before sucking the zesty sauce off of my hand. And when that isn't enough, I turn the bottle upside down over my mouth and squeeze until my throat burns with the rush of the tangy tomato taste.

I sit on one of our kitchen chairs, the uneven metal legs wobbling on the floor under my weight. The vinyl seat is torn, exposing the soft foam below. It feels warmer this way but I resist the urge to tear the rest of the vinyl off of the seat. It's both peaceful and scary being in this apartment alone, but I know I mustn't leave. I glance back at the window and the flakes drifting through the air.

And then there is the sound of footsteps echoing in the hall. Someone is approaching the apartment door. She's here! I smooth my hair and my dress frantically and suck in my breath, my heart pounding with anticipation.

The door opens with a thud and my mother stumbles in. Her hair is messy and she isn't wearing a coat, even though it's cold outside. I can smell the stench of vomit from the doorway. She teeters at the entrance before slamming the door behind her and swiping the hair from her face to better see where she is going. She is muttering, cursing under her breath, and wheezing from climbing the stairs to the apartment. I dangle my feet back and forth from the chair, eagerly awaiting her to notice me, when I see her glance around the room. She has the sickness again this morning. I can tell. She doesn't quite stand or walk or talk right and she looks like something else has taken over her body.

"Bernice!" she screams, even though I am in the same room, barely ten feet from where she's standing. She is carrying a plastic grocery bag, and although it isn't swelling, my tummy growls loudly. I am excited to see what she has brought.

"Right here, Mommy!" I say in my sweetest, brightest voice. She looks over at me and her eyes spring open with rage.

"What have you done?" she growls. I continue to smile, hoping that I've made her day, but she doesn't seem to like what I've done.

"I cleaned for you, Mommy!" I say. But my mother has made her way to the fridge, where shards of ceramic spill from behind it. The plate! Its pieces are coming out of hiding, tattling on me!

She picks up a few of the broken pieces and turns to me. "Damn you, kid," she spits, throwing the broken pieces across the room at me. I duck in fear, wondering how this could go so terribly wrong. She comes towards me, with her hands in the air until her grasp settles on my head. She grabs a fistful of my hair and yanks me off the chair, dragging me to the fridge.

"Clean this up," she bellows. The back of her hand hits me square in the mouth and I feel a sharp sting followed by the salty taste of blood. I nod in quick successions and bite my lip to keep from crying aloud. Tears cloud my vision and I try to sweep them as fast as they fall so that I can pick up all of the mess. I work quickly, tense at what might come next as she stands behind me.

When she is satisfied with what I've done, she drops the plastic bag in front of me. The bedroom door closes behind her and there is silence again. I dry my face on the front of my dress, certain that I am no longer beautiful, that I will never be good enough to make her happy. My body shivers with shame. I reach for the bag and open it, grateful at least to be able to satisfy my needy stomach. I know it won't be the meal I long for, the one I dream of having my mother lovingly prepare.

I hold my breath as I open the bag. Inside, I find a box of Strawberry Toaster Strudels, already opened and half eaten. They are soft and a bit soggy, but the sweet, fruity scent makes my mouth water. I fumble for the remaining pieces and stuff them furiously in my mouth. The flavourful filling dances on my tongue. I cannot eat them fast enough; I am desperate to calm the gnawing pains in my stomach. I'm wiping my sticky fingers on my dress, which is damp from my tears.

I approach the window again, but the flakes have stopped falling. I glance back down at the street, but the clean, fresh blanket of snow has been trampled upon, revealing dark tracks and dirty streets. Everything is messy and ugly now.

Chapter 3

Haywood House is a residential group home for girls just two blocks from the South Saskatchewan River, in the historic Saskatoon neighbourhood of City Park. Large, looming elm trees line the properties in this neighbourhood, and quaint, humble houses dot the street alongside larger, more impressive dwellings.

The government bought the old stately manor and had it renovated and retrofitted in 2001. Although it was originally meant for up to twelve girls, it currently houses seventeen.

The building itself is beautiful on the outside. Its tidy brick exterior and majestic columns tend to catch eyes from the street. Passersby can be found snapping photos of it, appreciating the grandeur and character of the old home. The grounds are immaculately kept, with flowers blooming throughout the season.

From the outside, it looks like the home of our dreams. Especially to any of us kids who have been through the system. Standing outside a building like this makes us wonder if we've come to the right place. After all, none of us ever expected we'd be pulling up to a house like this and settling down for the night, calling it home.

But once you get inside, the place starts to feel more like an institution than a home. Like even though the powers-that-be tried really hard to make it warm and cozy, by the time they were done with the outside, there wasn't anything left for the inside. Or maybe that's the trick of all these places. Make them seem really great at first glance so that the ones in charge can pat themselves on the back, so we kids can feel important when we pull up. Let the world think that good is being done. Just don't step inside. It's all downhill from there.

As you enter the house there's a small sitting room with two large, wing-backed chairs and a round wooden coffee table with magazines. The magazines are dog-eared and worn, issues of *Chatelaine* and *Canadian Living* from four years ago, yet we girls read them any chance we get. Sheena calls them "old lady" magazines. I read through them, even though the lives and stories inside seem so foreign to me. But instead of feeling sadness, I am fascinated. I see the confident women posing in the fashion pages, the delectable recipes, the craft projects and home décor ideas, and somehow, I have this feeling in my gut, like a fire burning in my belly. It's like if I concentrate enough, I can feel it all, taste it, and see it, like it's my life after all.

Beyond the sitting room is the front office. Lorna is the office manager. She answers the phones and takes all of the deliveries. She also does intake for Haywood. For any new kids coming in, Lorna is the first person they talk to.

After the office is a long corridor. There are offices, supply rooms, and a first aid station. The mint green walls and grey tiled floor make it seem like a hospital or clinic. There are charts on the walls, motivational slogans, and framed photos of events from past years, but I'm not sure that anyone has ever really looked at them.

This is where you find Betty's office. She's the counsellor here and she helps put broken kids together again. I credit her with saving me from myself. When I came here I was so full of pain, I had no idea how to release it. Betty showed me ways to cope and deal with everything that had happened to me.

From there you enter the cafeteria, a room that smells more of antiseptic and bleach than of delectable cooking, even though the food here is pretty good. The metal chairs are all lined up perfectly around the wooden tables until the bell rings for the next meal.

The washrooms and sleeping quarters are just past the cafeteria. Having to push through heavy double doors to get to your bed hardly conjures up a feeling of hominess, but it's alright. All of our beds are lined up, five to a row. Each of us has a metal headboard, a foam mattress, a lump of a pillow, a sheet, and a wool blanket, as well as a small metal bedside table with a drawer and a lamp. The bulb in the lamp is so dim that I can barely read anything when it's on. I guess it wouldn't be so great if all of us had bright lights on while others tried to sleep. Privacy is a pretty foreign concept here.

Today's a big day at Haywood. We're saying goodbye to Mandy. She's twelve and has only been here for a month or so. She's pretty. She has long black hair, clear brown skin, and she's petite. She's been one of the quieter ones here, but she fit in nicely.

It's never easy when one of the girls leaves. We don't know who to expect next and what she'll be like, like when Analise came last year with her flippant attitude and the idea that she'd be running the place. She was only fifteen at the time, thinking she knew everything and that we'd be bowing down to her. But that's not how it was. Some of us have been in here for what feels like forever and the ways of this place, the roles … they've all been established. Some fresh-faced newcomer can't come in here calling the shots.

I guess we all come angry, tough, out to prove something, but we never really get the chance. We're expected to just step into place in this new environment and its rules like puppets or robots, participating, going through the motions. Emotions get buried. Eventually you get to feeling numb, dead inside. Or maybe we are dead inside before we even come. That's more like my story. But for me, coming here felt like salvation.

Once you come to Haywood House, chances are you're here for a while. Most of us girls have been in the system for years and are now permanent wards. And here's the newsflash no one seems to care about: when you are a teenager, you aren't getting adopted. There's no line-up of parents eagerly combing the building, ready to light up at the sight of their beloved chosen one, the missing piece of the puzzle that will make their family complete. I used to lie awake at night and dream of the possibility that someone somewhere would see me, truly see me, and decide that I was worth taking a chance on.

Mandy is one of the lucky ones. An aunt she's never met lives on Thunderchild First Nation, a reserve two and a half hours north of Saskatoon, and has agreed to be her guardian, a "PSI," or "Person Having a Sufficient Interest in the Child," which means that Mandy's going to be with family and may get her better life after all. Even though we don't know Mandy that well, we're all really happy for her. *She's still young,* I think to myself. *She still has a chance.*

The staff at Haywood is planning a little celebration for her. There will be cake after supper and we'll all get to say our goodbyes. Mandy seems excited and hopeful. Her aunt will be picking her up in the morning. She packed her few belongings hours ago, and she's been pacing and staring out the window a lot.

"You okay?" I ask her.

She turns to me and smiles nervously.

"I think so," she says, biting her lip. "I'm scared, Andy."

Her eyes well up with tears. I give her a squeeze and try to reassure her. Being the oldest one here now, I think the younger ones look up to me. It seems weird to look up to someone who has had the life I've had. After all, it hasn't worked out so well for me, has it? This definitely isn't where I saw myself at seventeen. But I like Mandy. I wish her well and I want her story to be different.

"It'll be great, Mandy …" I say, wanting it to be true for her. "You're going to a real home. A real life," I remind her. After all, for all that Haywood House is — it's not really a home.

She nods, lost in thought, her gaze fixated on something I can't see. And yet I'm nervous for her. I find myself biting my nails and pacing, too.

That night, Gertie, the night supervisor, whistles loudly to get our attention amidst the loud chatter of the supper hour. She has wheeled in a cart that has a plain, slab cake on top. She's got a wide grin on her face, as though she can barely contain her excitement at the prospect of giving us cake. She waits for the room to quiet before speaking.

"Ladies," she starts, "You all know we are saying goodbye to a very special young woman tonight. Mandy, we will miss you and we wish you all the best." Gertie smiles, and to our surprise, her voice cracks with emotion. The response from the tables is mixed. Some of the younger girls are crying and clutching each other at the thought of saying goodbye, while others are rolling their eyes and chuckling at Gertie. Either way, it's hard to know how to feel. Girls like us aren't good at trusting people anymore. And lots of girls come and go here at Haywood. It makes it hard to get attached to someone or have a friend here sometimes.

Early the next morning, the sounds of the building begin to wake us. Groans from the boiler room and the subsequent rattling of the radiators springing to life send vibrations through the walls. The shuffling feet of the staff across the tiled floor and the beeps and muffled phrases coming from the staff radios all rouse us from our sleep. I open my eyes slowly, adjusting to the light in the room. Some of the girls are up already; I turn over, not quite ready to face the day.

"Why did she just go like that?" I hear Analise whisper. She's the number one gossip, always hungry for the newest developments around here. Curious, I turn back around in my bed and see her huddled with Lisa and Monica. I wonder who they are talking about and what's going on. I sit up in my bed and rub the sleep from my eyes.

"She told me she didn't want to make anyone feel bad," Lisa says. "She didn't want us to see her leave, knowing that we have to stay." And I realize that they are talking about Mandy and that she is already gone. I look over at her bed, stripped down to the foam mattress, no indication that she was ever there.

"Good luck, Mandy," I whisper to myself. "I hope you make it." And with that, I lay back down into the bed, willing myself to sleep. I want to dream of Mandy and her new homecoming, of an aunt who welcomes her with open arms and radiates love. I want to believe that she's found the home she's been longing for.

Chapter 4

School is mandatory at Haywood, no exceptions. Even when Christal got knocked up by her slimy boyfriend, she was back at school two days after her baby's birth.

Most of us walk to the alternative school. The classes are smaller, and the teachers are more understanding. It's not as structured as the regular system, so we can learn at our own pace. I like school. I enjoy the challenge, and I like the socializing.

In my younger years I rarely got in trouble and did well in school. I wasn't one of those kids who begged to take a day off of school or pretended to be sick to avoid going. I never wanted to miss a day of school because I could be assured that a day at home would be far worse than anything school had to offer.

I could always count on eating at school too, whether it was from stealing snacks from the lunch kits lined up in the lockers by being the last to go out for recess, or by sneaking back to the classroom during library or gym. I often found myself quickly stuffing whatever food I could find in my mouth, barely stopping to chew.

I didn't want to steal, but I was so hungry, it felt like my stomach was forcing me to do it to keep it quiet and calm. As long as I took only one thing from a lunch or two, it usually went unnoticed. Most of the kids barely cared about what they brought or had no idea what their parents had packed to notice anything missing.

There were a few occasions where I'd look in horror as some of the pickier eaters threw perfectly good food in the garbage, anxious to get outside for recess. I'd wait until everyone had cleared out before reaching in and retrieving it. Sometimes if I'd collected enough food, I'd wrap my findings up carefully and save it in my locker so that the next day I could pull out a regular lunch like everyone else. I was never caught.

My teachers were always good to me, almost too good. I remember as a young kid I'd try to stay late to help clean the classroom or just to talk. I'm not sure the teachers ever knew how much I depended on those inter-actions, how I'd savour every word and replay it in my mind. They made me feel like I mattered. Having some-one so interested in me and my life was intoxicating.

Mrs. Duggleman was my favourite. She was my grade four teacher. She smelled like apples and cinna-mon and had shimmery blonde hair and crystal blue eyes. She was regal looking, with a gentle voice and the softest hands I ever touched. I idolized her. I would sit in class, in rapt attention, hoping she'd call on me so that I could win her praise.

Mrs. Duggleman was married to a police officer. He was tall and handsome, and to me they made the perfect couple. I imagined their home being a mansion, immaculately kept. I imagined that she'd have pies baking and music playing in her kitchen, the sound of her laughter echoing through the home while her husband hugged her. I dreamed that one day Mrs. Duggleman would take me home with her and announce that I'd be theirs. It would be the perfect life.

Mr. and Mrs. Duggleman did not have any children. It was surprising to me because I thought they'd make the perfect parents. And anyone could see how much Mrs. Duggleman adored children. I figured she just loved us all too much that there wasn't room in her heart for anyone else.

Mrs. Duggleman was the first person who I felt really loved me. She was so kind to me that sometimes I would feel tears prick up by the sides of my eyelids, but I wasn't sure why. She just made me feel so good that I could burst.

She seemed to go out of her way to talk with me, even when we weren't in class. In class, she'd focus much of her attention on me, a look of kind concern in her eyes. She'd lend me her sweater on cold days when I'd come to school wearing tank tops in the middle of winter.

"Bernice, honey," she'd say. "Why don't you use my sweater to keep your arms warm today?" And I'd beam with pride that she'd chosen me.

The year I had Mrs. Duggleman I stole less from the other kids' lunches because she'd make up some story about how both she and her husband had made her a lunch, so somehow she had two, and food couldn't go to waste, could it? I knew that wasn't the truth, but I was too hungry to care. Her lunches were the best. I'd usually get a sandwich on really soft bread. It would have all of the fixings: turkey or ham, lettuce, tomato, cheese, and the tangy taste of mustard and mayonnaise. It was the freshest thing I'd ever tasted and the layers of flavour seemed to burst in my mouth with every bite. She always had cookies in her lunch too, which confirmed my assumption that she baked homemade goodies in her home all the time. Even the carrots or apples tasted amazing; so crisp and fresh and nourishing.

I wasn't embarrassed about Mrs. Duggleman pretending she'd had two lunches packed for herself in order to feed me. To me, it just reaffirmed our special relationship. She was always checking to see how I was doing, if there was anything I needed. She would often ask me about my mom and about how things were at home. I told her everything was fine because *that* was what I was embarrassed about.

Sometimes Mrs. Duggleman would be deep in conversation with the principal or another lady at the school. They'd stand close together, talking in hushed tones, glancing my way. I knew they must be talking about me, but I couldn't understand why. I'd always done a good job at hiding my home life, or at least I thought so. I didn't want Mrs. Duggleman to have any idea about Jacqueline, so I made excuses for her absences at parent-teacher interviews and pretended she was a model mother. When things would get so bad at home that even I was tired of trying to make her out to be a good mother, I clammed up at the mention of her. I was good at deflecting the conversation. After all, any attention to what was going on at home would only make things worse. No one could know the reality of life outside of school, or I'd be in for it for sure. Jacqueline would give me a beating I'd never forget.

Then one morning towards the end of the school year, I arrived much earlier than any of the other students. I decided to sit in the classroom and enjoy the peace and quiet before everyone else arrived. I shuffled my way down the hall towards the blackened classroom and reached my hand up to turn on the lights.

In the seconds before the lights were turned on, I heard a soft sob in the darkness. When the lights came on, I was shocked to see Mrs. Duggleman's head lying on her desk with her head in her hands. She was cradling the phone receiver in her shoulder but she was crying so hard that whoever was on the other line must have been having a hard time understanding what she was saying.

"I thought it was …" She hiccupped. "There was so much blood … the baby … I'll never be a mother … all I do is kill them …" and after a few heavy sobs, she went on. "It's happened five times … what is wrong with me?"

And then in that instant, she seemed to notice that her surroundings had changed, that someone had turned on the lights, and that she wasn't alone. She looked up, panic-stricken, her face puffy, and her eyes swollen and red. She gasped and quickly regained her composure.

"I've gotta go," she stammered into the phone and quickly replaced the receiver. She stood up abruptly, knocking the chair to the ground. Smoothing her skirt and her face, she smiled at me. I felt awful. Watching Mrs. Duggleman cry felt like daggers in my heart. I couldn't bear to see her in such pain. I felt angry at myself for coming to school and stumbling upon something I knew I wasn't meant to see. I didn't even know what her pain meant.

"Oh, my dear Bernice…" she said, coming towards me with her arms outstretched. "Good morning to you," she said in her sing-song voice. I gave her the strongest hug I could, hoping it would help her feel better. She squeezed me tighter than usual and smoothed my hair.

"Come on in, sweetheart." She smiled.

Confused, I looked up at her face, at the sadness in her eyes and blurted, "Are you killing babies, Mrs. Duggleman?" She looked at me in horror and blinked back tears.

"Oh, sweetie, Mrs. Duggleman was talking about grown-up stuff. Nobody is killing babies," she said softly. "I was hoping to have a baby and become a mommy," she said slowly. I nodded to show her I understood and that it was okay to tell me more. "But for some reason, a baby can't grow in my tummy like it can for other mommies." She tried to smile to reassure me, but all I could see was sadness. "I'm not sure why this happens and it makes me feel very sad," she went on.

Then, as though she felt she'd said too much, she smiled brightly. "But I have all of my students and I love you all very much," she said, giving me another squeeze. "I am very lucky!"

But all I could think was that if she wanted to be a mommy and babies couldn't grow in her tummy, then she wasn't lucky at all. And how could the kindest, most beautiful woman in the world not be a mommy when she'd be the best mommy in the world?

And then I was angry at myself because the thought of Mrs. Duggleman having a baby filled me with jealousy. If she had a baby, then she wouldn't be at school and then I wouldn't have her and then what? I imagined her kissing and snuggling a cooing baby and the thought was almost more than I could bear. Could someone wishing for something with all their might be destroyed by someone else who wished it not to happen with all of their might too? I was filled with guilt and shame at the very thought of my jealousy.

After that day, things changed between the two of us. Mrs. Duggleman asked me how I was doing more often than before. She seemed to pay more attention to me than usual. I'd glance at her and catch her staring at me with concern in her eyes. I knew we shared a special secret after that morning in the classroom. I never mentioned what had happened to anyone. I wanted it to be our private moment. I'm pretty sure she wished I hadn't seen her crying like that, but knowing that she was in pain only deepened my love for her.

I wrote kind letters to her and put them on her desk. I drew colourful scenes of the two of us holding hands in the park. I thought of all the other kids I'd seen give drawings to their parents, then watch as they waited excitedly for a proud reaction. I felt the same way when I gave them to Mrs. Duggleman. In my eyes, if she couldn't have a baby, I was more than willing to step up and be her child.

Then one afternoon in early June, towards the end of the school year, the weather was unseasonably hot. The temperature soared to 34 degrees Celsius and without air conditioning, the school was sweltering. Students were wiping sweat from their brows and squirming uncomfortably in their seats. It was too hot to concentrate.

I had come to school that morning with fresh bruises and cuts. My mother had beat me with a belt and thrown me in the bathtub the night before. Her boyfriend had broken up with her and left her for another woman. When Jacqueline came home, she was steaming. One look at her shaking with rage and I knew I was in for it.

Sure enough, she came at me immediately, anxious to unleash her anger. After repeated swings of the belt on my back and legs, blood began to seep from the stinging wounds. She continued until she was panting, depleted. I felt like I was on fire. She picked me up by the arms and dragged me to the bathroom, throwing me into the bathtub before turning on the hot water full blast. I yelped in pain, knowing that I would soon be scalded. She laughed at my yelp, satisfied with what she'd done. She turned off the water and left the room, humming as though nothing had happened. I curled into a ball, clutching my legs as close as I could to my body. Each wound felt like flames jumping off my body, eager to find relief.

The next morning, my nightgown had stuck in my dried wounds. I had to peel it carefully and many of the cuts reopened and oozed. I winced and wiped tears as I tried to remove my pajamas. I looked in the mirror and gasped at the reflection of myself. How could I go to school like this? How would I hide these awful marks?

I pulled on the biggest T-shirt I had, hoping it would be loose enough to minimize the pain, but my arms were mottled with bright red evidence. I searched for a sweatshirt and pulled it carefully over the T-shirt, wincing at every stretch.

There I was, on the hottest day of the year, almost faint with heat because of all the layers of clothes I was wearing. I moved slowly all day, feigning illness so that I didn't have to participate in gym class and move around too much or risk bumping into anyone. As the day progressed, I started getting dizzy. I couldn't concentrate in class. Sweat poured down my back, the salt stinging and occupying my every thought. I was flushed and lightheaded.

"Bernice, why on earth are you wearing so many clothes, my dear?" Mrs. Duggleman asked. "It's sweltering outside! Why don't you take your sweatshirt off before you get heat stroke?" The other children had long since shed any layers of clothing and most were wearing tank tops, shorts, and sandals.

"I'm okay, Mrs. Duggleman," I assured her. "It's not too bad."

She didn't seem convinced. She lifted my hair off of my neck, the bottom layers slick with sweat. Even my toes squished in sweat in my socks and running shoes. Mrs. Duggleman sighed and made her way out of the classroom.

Fifteen minutes later, she returned and called my name. She took me by the hand and led me out of the classroom. I figured she was taking me to be her special helper for something, but when we got down the hallway and stopped at the conference room, I knew that wasn't the case. She guided me into the room, where the principal and the lady Mrs. Duggleman often whispered to, were sitting waiting for our arrival. They smiled warmly at me and welcomed me into the room, but at once I felt very uncomfortable. I looked up at Mrs. Duggleman, a little scared and unsure.

"It's going to be alright," she assured me, and together we sat down.

"I'm Debby," the lady said, holding out her hand for me to shake. "I'm the school social worker." My stomach began to flip-flop and I felt dizzy and sick. I could sense that this wasn't going to be good.

"We want to talk to you about how things are going at home," she continued. I looked up at Mrs. Duggleman who looked very sad, but was nodding at me to answer. "We have been concerned about some things that we have noticed here at school and we'd just like to discuss these things to make sure that everything is alright," Debby said kindly.

The room started spinning and the adults' heads were blurry and their words didn't make any sense anymore, and I didn't know what to do.

"It's okay, honey," I heard Mrs. Duggleman say. I felt her hand rubbing my back. I wanted to cry out in pain, but Mrs. Duggleman didn't know, couldn't know, why it hurt so badly. Tears began to spill from my eyes. What could I say? Their eyes were all on me, watching me squirm uncomfortably in my seat. My face felt hot and my lips quivered. I felt like I had lost control over myself. I didn't know what I was doing, why I was going to do it, but the next thing I did was tell them everything. Everything.

They looked at me with wide eyes while I spoke. I don't know why I couldn't stop, why the words kept tumbling out faster and faster. And when I was done, Mrs. Duggleman was wiping tears from her eyes. Instinctively, I knew I wasn't in any trouble, but that somehow things were going to be different for me. Mrs. Duggleman wiped her cheeks with a tissue and blew her nose, and then she hugged me tight. I secretly hoped it meant that Mrs. Duggleman would take me home and take care of me just like I imagined.

They told me to stay seated in the room while they left to discuss what we'd talked about and to make some phone calls. Every minute in that room felt like hours, my knees knocking together with fear as I realized what I had just done. I held my breath when the door to that little conference room swung open. It was Mrs. Duggleman, greeting me with a sad smile. "You did the right thing, sweetheart," she said, putting her arms around me. But my head throbbed and my stomach wrenched with uncertainty.

I wasn't sure if it was the right thing at all.

That day would be my last day with my mother. I never went home again.

Chapter 5

It's usually pretty quiet around here, so when security is called to the front at seven in the morning, something big is going on.

"Guys, check this out!" Lisa calls out. Monica, Analise, and I jump out of bed to follow her. We creep down the hallway and peer through the glass panes in the door to get a look at what's happening. The source of the trouble is a pixie of a girl, about the size of a nine-year-old but by her face I can tell she's older. She stands glaring at Betty and Madge and Phyllis, two of Haywood's security staff. Madge and Phyllis are tough to contend with, but most of the time we make their job pretty easy. The few encounters with them that I'd witnessed over the years had been enough for me to make sure we never needed to cross paths.

"That's what the fuss is all about?" Monica says, rolling her eyes. "Oh, please! Like, what is *she* going to do?" A couple of the girls laugh and decide the scene isn't worth watching. They turn and head back to bed. The rest of us are grateful for the extra room so we can catch a better glimpse. I have to admit, she's pretty tiny, this one. We're all a bit puzzled as to what she thinks she's going to do with all these people around her, and Madge and Phyllis look ready for whatever she wants to dish out.

"Don't you even think about touching me," the girl warns. Madge and Phyllis stand on either side of her, clearly not intimidated. The girl's eyes are blazing; her fists are clenched and ready to strike. Her head is shaved, black stubble peppering the white of her scalp. She wears no makeup except for heavy black eyeliner and to me she looks like a corpse. Dressed in a frayed denim skirt which barely covers her bum, torn fishnet stockings, and combat boots, she looks the part of someone who doesn't give a crap about what anyone thinks of her.

"Okay Trina, let's get in and get settled," Madge says sternly. She reaches for the girl's elbow to guide her through the office and Trina jumps back in alarm.

"Cut the drama, honey," Phyllis smirks.

"Screw you." Trina spits, her saliva hitting Phyllis square in the face. Phyllis wipes it with the back of her hand and pretends it never happened.

"Let's go, honey," Phyllis says softly. "You can make this easy or you can make this difficult, but either way you're here." Trina sticks her tongue out at her and gives her a shove. Madge steps in, taking her by the arm.

"I don't have to be here if I don't want to," Trina says. "And I sure as hell don't have to stay." She straightens her skirt and pulls it down. I'm not a rocket scientist, but anyone can see that if she dares sit down, the bottom of that skirt would sit at her hips.

"Trina, dear, come with me and we'll get you settled," Betty says gently. Trina glares at her but follows. Knowing we shouldn't be spying, we all stand up straight.

"Get back to your beds or head for breakfast, girls," Madge barks at us. We turn on our heels, scurrying back down the hallway. We all giggle and head back to our room.

"She seems like a real winner," Analise says.

"And what's with her hair and that outfit? Yikes," Monica remarks.

"We get her instead of Mandy? Great ..." Analise says sarcastically.

All of us girls start on our morning chores before heading to the cafeteria for breakfast. Eggs, toast, and fruit are on the menu this morning, and my stomach jumps at the sight. I love breakfast. It is my favourite meal of the day. Living at Haywood has given me three square meals a day and I have never missed one. I make sure to eat whatever is made. Even a basic bowl of cheerios with its delicate crunch and hint of sweetness mixed with cold, creamy milk is a culinary delight to me.

I eagerly scoop bits of egg and the flowing yolk onto my fork and follow it with a bite of warm toast. "This is *so* good," I breathe. The others look over at me and laugh.

"Andy and her food," Lisa says, shaking her head. She sits perfectly straight in her chair, her hair and makeup artfully applied. Lisa is obsessed with her appearance. She is rail thin and picks at her food, eating tiny bits at a time, and chewing them for several minutes before swallowing. She always looks at me in disgust when I eat, and sometimes I eat more than I feel like eating just so I can get a reaction from her.

The girls are always teasing me about how much I eat, how I can't wait for the next meal. We make small talk while I start on my orange.

"Look!" Analise says, pointing. "That girl is here."

Phyllis is guiding her down to the cafeteria for breakfast.

"Girls," Phyllis announces. "This is Trina Baxter. As many of you know, she has just joined us this morning. I hope you all help her to feel welcome here."

Trina does not look up at us. Her arms are crossed in front of her. Phyllis points to the stack of trays and the food buffet, but Trina simply scoffs at her and turns away. She stomps over to an empty table and glances over at the rest of us briefly before pulling out a chair and slumping down into it. She doesn't move for a half an hour.

"What is her deal?" Lisa says, shaking her head. "Chill already." She snickers.

Does Lisa forget that we all come in here angry? None of us come in here happy. How could we? I don't know what it is about her, but Trina is interesting to me. I wonder what has brought her here, what her story is. The other girls chat happily and get up to leave for school.

"Are you coming?" Lisa asks me. I look over at Trina, who is sitting motionless. Her eyes remain fixed on a spot on the floor. I feel the urge to go and talk to her, to let her know it isn't so bad here, but then I decide against it.

"Yeah, I'm coming," I reply.

I follow behind Lisa but turn briefly to Trina and say, "Hey." To my surprise, she actually breaks her gaze and looks at me for a second before returning to whatever she is looking at. I make it to the end of the hallway and glance back one last time, but Trina has resumed her fixation on the spot on the floor. Her resistance to being here reminds me of myself. How every new placement, and every new place to sleep, felt wrong, how it had never really felt like home — except for one.

Maybe the feeling of home is something none of us will ever truly feel. Maybe we're destined to roam the world like vagabonds, never settling down in one place too long. Maybe we'll never carve out a place of our own.

Chapter 6

June 2003

After the meeting with the social worker, the principal, and Mrs. Duggleman, I am taken to the principal's office. I sit, shaking with fear. I have no idea what is going to happen to me. I have no idea where I am going and I don't know what my mother will do to me when she finds out what I have done. I feel sick, sorry that I have told them anything.

When the door to the principal's office finally swings open, it's Mrs. Duggleman. She says she can't stay with me because she has to return to class, but she puts her arms around me again and kneels in front of me so that our eyes are level. "Bernice, honey," she says softly, tears spilling down her cheeks. "You are going to be safe now," she assures me. "No one will hurt you. I want you to know that you are very strong and very special." She wipes her face with the back of her hand and then reaches for another tissue to blow her nose. "You be a brave girl, okay?"

I nod and hug her tight, breathing in her comforting scent. She steps out of the office. I've never loved anyone as much as I love her. If Mrs. Duggleman says it's going to be okay, then I believe her.

Minutes later, Debby, the social worker, and two other ladies pack me into a van. I have no idea where we are going. Everyone seems to be talking around me or talking about me, but no one ever explains what is happening. After a visit to the hospital and what seems like endless visits from strangers examining me, taking pictures, and asking questions, I am finally put back into the van.

We drive for what feels like hours. I am tired, hungry, and scared. I sit in the back seat, my fingers twisting the cuffs of my shirt nervously. My stomach wrenches from not knowing where we are going. The ladies in the front seat talk about the weather and the traffic as though I'm not even here. We turn onto a crescent with stately elms looming over the street. It is lush and beautiful. I study each home as we drive by. The street is lined with well-kept homes. There are flowers and sprinklers in the yards. Some people are mowing lawns, a sight I've only seen on television. I might as well be on a different planet. This is a picture-perfect neighbourhood, straight out of the pages of a book.

The van comes to an abrupt stop in front of a simple, but pretty little house. A low wrought iron fence surrounds the property. Flowers line the walkway; a welcome sign is perfectly centred on the front of the doorway.

"This is where you'll be staying," the social worker says. It's the first time she's spoken to me directly since we started driving. She puts the vehicle in park and unbuckles her seatbelt. I stare at the house, and my knees start to tremble. I can feel my breathing getting all ragged and weird, like I'm about to pass out. The ladies hold open the door and wait for me to step out. I feel a sense of impending doom.

How else am I supposed to feel? What will these people be like? Are they nice? Do other children live here? How long do I have to stay? Will I be here forever? The questions tumble through my mind one after the other. I'm confused and scared.

"Come on, Bernice ... it'll be fine," she says, but it sounds more like she's trying to get me out of the van so she can move on with her day than anything else. I step out onto the pavement. The trembling has spread from my knees to my entire body but I feel comfort in the warmth of the sun. I shuffle to the door, cowering behind the two ladies. The chime of the doorbell brings approaching footsteps.

"Hello! Please come in!" a woman greets us, full of cheer. She's breathtakingly beautiful with long blonde hair that falls in bouncy waves from her shoulders. She's wearing soft makeup and has thick eyelashes that outline her enormous blue eyes. She reminds me of Mrs. Duggleman.

"And who are you, my dear?" she asks me gently. I must look like I've seen a ghost, standing there trembling, my eyes wide open in fear.

"B-b-b ... Bernice," I manage.

"I'm pleased to meet you, Bernice! I'm Shelley." She looks to the ladies who are all watching me, smiling.

We all enter into the living room and I look around at the surroundings. There are leather couches and marble tables. The carpet is so plush that my toes almost get lost from view, and it's white, of all colours. It's such a beautiful, clean home. A big-screen TV takes up a corner of the room. I've never seen anything like it. The images dance upon the screen in perfect clarity, and I'm mesmerized by the colours and size. Pictures in fancy silver frames line the walls. Most of the pictures are of adults, but there are a couple of frames with photos of two young children. I wonder who they are, if they live here too. I've never had brothers or sisters before.

"Why don't I show you Bernice's room?" Shelley offers. We all follow her down the hallway. She turns the handle of the door and the door swings wide open. "This is your room, my dear," she says to me. I try not to show any emotion, but inside I'm flabbergasted.

It's a room fit for a princess. There is pale pink wallpaper with tiny pink and green flowers on the walls. The same plush carpet in the living room is in this room too. A huge canopy bed is thick with layers of bedding, all in pink and soft green to match the wallpaper. A white lamp with a pretty patterned shade adorns the white bedside table. There is a dresser against the longest wall and a bookcase in the corner that are both painted white. The bookcase is filled with books of all sizes. Frilly curtains in the same shade of soft green cover the window. It's almost magical in here. The thought that is where I will sleep is almost too much for me to handle. I glance around in wonder, trying to keep my jaw from hanging open.

"Will this be okay?" Shelley kneels down and asks me. I nod, biting my lip. It's a beautiful room, far more beautiful than I could ever imagine. But the bigger question on my mind is whether or not living here will be okay.

"Why don't you get settled while the rest of us talk?" the social worker says. She hands me my backpack and motions for the other women to head back to the living room.

My backpack. It's all I have at the moment. No clothes, no other shoes, no other belongings. Even my backpack is worn and dirty. I'm afraid to set it down on this white carpet, afraid that one false move will have me out on the street or somewhere worse. I mustn't do anything to make Shelley angry with me. I hear the muffled conversation of the women in the other room and I decide to step forward to examine the contents of the bookcase. There are dozens of books on every shelf, shiny new books that look like they've never been read. My heart jumps at the sight.

I've always loved reading. The ability to escape and get lost in someone else's story is thrilling. I'm comforted by the sight of all of these books and the possibility that I may get to read them. I sit on the edge of the bed peering around the room in wonder. I'm interrupted by the sound of someone calling my name. I quickly stand and make my way down the hallway where the women are.

"Bathe her right away," Debby says quietly. "And watch for lice." She stops talking as soon as I appear and smiles. "Bernice, it is time for us to go now. Mr. and Mrs. Thiessen will take good care of you." And just like that, the front door closes behind them, leaving me and Shelley Thiessen alone.

"I know this must be so hard for you, Bernice," Shelley says. "My husband Luke will be home soon and you will meet him too," she says awkwardly. I stand in silence, nodding. "We will go out and get you some more things, my poor dear. Some new outfits, some new shoes, and other things you will need."

I don't know what to say. I have no idea what this all means. Am I staying here forever? Will I never see Jacqueline or my home again? How will I get all these new things? Do I call her Shelley? Is she my new mom?

"Why don't we get you cleaned up?" she says. I immediately stiffen. "I can run a nice hot bubble bath for you," she says. She walks down the hallway and pulls out a thick, plush towel from the linen closet and enters the bathroom. Sitting on the edge of the bathtub, she turns on the faucet and then pours in a silky liquid from a bottle. From where I stand I can smell the fruity aroma of the suds and see the steam starting to rise from the tub. I start to feel my knees knock together again.

Shelley is humming and rearranging toiletries, seemingly oblivious to the terror I feel. She sets a neatly folded towel on the edge of the sink, within easy reach of the bathtub.

"It's almost done." She waits for another minute or so before turning the faucet off. Then she says, "It's all ready, Bernice."

But I'm frozen on the spot and I don't know what to do. My entire body is trembling. Once she realizes that I'm not coming, Shelley turns towards me, her smile slipping from her face.

"It's okay, honey," she says. "Nobody is going to hurt you. Let's just get you cleaned up and you'll feel much better." Sensing that I'm not sure how to proceed, she adds, "You get in and get comfortable and I'll just check on you to make sure you're alright in a few minutes, okay? Just call me if there is anything you need."

I nod, hesitating for a moment before entering the bathroom.

"There is shampoo on the ledge of the bathtub and soap in the little dish. Will you need help washing your hair?" she asks. I shake my head no and timidly shut the door behind me.

Shelley has no idea how long I've been washing my hair all by myself. Often we'd go days without water and I'd be unable to bathe. When I started to smell, I'd try to wash up in the girls washroom at school, hoping no one would come in and see me. I'd cup my hands together and fill them with water under the tap, quickly tossing the water on my hair before it seeped through my fingers. I'd run globs of liquid soap from the dispenser down my arms and through my hair before cupping my hands again to rinse. Then I'd kneel below the hand dryer, hoping the burst of air would dry my hair so that no one would notice. I'd pray that no one would walk in and see me. It usually took four tries under the hand dryer to dry my hair enough.

I undress quickly and wiggle down into the tub, wincing in pain. My wounds are stinging but the heat of the water is comforting. The bathroom is all white and spotless. There is not a speck of dirt or dust to be seen. This is what I imagined Mrs. Duggleman's house to be like, I realize. I breathe deeply, inhaling the intoxicating scent of the bubbles and I feel my muscles start to relax. I squeeze a huge glob of shampoo into my open palm, the fruity smelling liquid trailing down my forearm. I want to be sure that I smell nice for them, that I'm all clean.

A few minutes later, Shelley knocks at the door and asks if she can come in. I straighten and tense up again, but I'm mostly covered in bubbles so I say yes.

She gasps when she sees the marks on my body, but then composes herself.

"Are you doing okay?" she asks. "Do you need anything?" I politely tell her no. "May I take these and wash them?" she asks. Before I can protest she scoops up my sweaty clothes and sets some clean clothing down on the floor. I breathe a sigh of relief as she closes the door softly behind her. I sink down into the water to rinse the shampoo from my hair.

A moment later I hear voices, and I realize Shelley's husband must be home. I quickly stand up from the tub and reach for the towel. It is so thick that it feels like a blanket and I long to wrap myself in it fully, but even the pillowy threads of cotton aren't soft enough against the stinging wounds.

I unfold the outfit that Shelley has brought in and quickly try it on. I'm without underwear, but the pants are a soft, fleecy material and feel comfortable nonetheless. I slip the plain T-shirt over my head. It feels great to be so clean and to smell so good.

"Oh, Bernice, you're out!" Shelley remarks when she sees me standing in the hallway. My hair is dripping down my back, forming a large wet circle on the back of my shirt. "Luke!" she calls. "Come and meet Bernice!"

A handsome man dressed in a suit rounds the corner. He's got a wide smile and holds out his hand for me to shake. I do so, a bit apprehensive.

"Hi, Bernice," he says, his voice deep. "My name is Luke. I've brought home an early supper for us. I thought you might be hungry." For once, I can't help but smile. I'm famished and I can smell whatever he's brought. My stomach is grumbling.

I follow them into their kitchen and dining room, both exquisitely decorated and clean. There are two pizza boxes sitting on the countertop and Shelley has set the table with plates and napkins. She's put out a jug of milk and three kinds of juices. I quickly scoop up a couple of slices of pizza and finish them before Luke and Shelley have filled their plates. They look over at me in surprise but say nothing.

After the meal, Shelley asks if I'd like to go shopping. On our way out, she glances down at my running shoes, which are ratty and worn. She makes a remark about getting new shoes too.

We arrive at a huge mall, the size of several city blocks. There are quite a few shoppers, many of them well dressed. We pass a teenage girl who is holding up a hanger with a pretty blue dress on it in front of her chest. She asks for her friend's opinion. "I wouldn't be caught dead in that!" Her friend tells her. I chew on my lower lip as we pass, feeling embarrassed because I like the dress a lot.

"I was just joking around," the girl holding the dress says. "It is pretty ugly." But I can tell her from the look on her face that she secretly likes the dress too. She shoves it onto the rack and follows her friend.

When we get to the girls' section, I see mothers with what must be their daughters combing through the racks. Some of the girls gush over items, while others stand bored and ready to leave. I've never been shopping before, and certainly not with my mother. The only clothes or shoes I remember getting are hand-me-downs, even though I had no idea who they were handed down from, and they were often ill-fitting and stained.

Shelley is grabbing things left and right. She holds the items up to my chest to get a feel for my size. "How about this?" she asks. "Or what about this?"

I don't know what to say. To me, it is all beautiful. Everything looks so clean and perfect.

In just over an hour, Shelley has bought me a dozen new outfits, socks, underwear, five pairs of pajamas, three pairs of shoes, and a jacket. She has also bought a bag of accessories: headbands, hair elastics, necklaces, and bracelets.

She is practically giggling with excitement at purchasing all of this, while I stand in stunned silence at the checkout counter. I can't wrap my mind around how much money this must have cost and how she hasn't even blinked an eye. It's hard to imagine that these things are for me.

"Isn't this fun?" she says to me. I give her a small smile, realizing that this is what other girls must do with their mothers. "Bernice, I hope you're alright with this," Shelley says, fumbling to hold all of the bags. "This will do for now, right?" she asks. She's looking to me for reassurance as though I may feel differently. I've never owned this many beautiful things before. I'm not sure that I deserve them, or that I can accept them. We step onto the pavement of the parking lot and I follow her to the car.

"It's all so amazing," I manage to say, but then a giant sob wells in my throat and bursts through. I start crying uncontrollably. Shelley immediately gets down on her knees and envelopes me in a close hug.

"Oh, honey, it's going to be alright," she says gripping me tighter. I cry until I start to hiccup. Shelley pulls a tissue from her purse and helps me wipe my tears. "Let's go home," she says.

I feel overwhelming gratitude for Shelley and what she's already done for me. I put my hand in hers as we make our way through the parking lot, feeling like we could be like any regular mother and daughter, shopping and spending time together. Maybe Mrs. Duggleman was right. Maybe, just maybe, this could be home.

Chapter 7

It's Sunday afternoon at Haywood. That means we are usually gathered in the cafeteria room, playing cards or board games or doing homework in time for class on Monday. They call it "quiet time," like we're babies all over again. Lisa and I are playing a game of UNO, though neither of us is really into it.

"Did you hear about Trina?" Lisa says, lowering her voice.

"No," I reply.

"She's leaving tonight. She's not coming back."

"What do you mean?" I ask. "Where is she going?"

Trina has hardly spoken to anyone since she's been here. She hasn't lost her trademark glare yet, either.

"Girls, you should be going to talk to her," Gertie had chided us. But each of us had been trying and she'd barely acknowledged us. What was the point? If she wanted to be like that, let her.

Lisa leans in closer. "I heard her boyfriend is picking her up later tonight, but she's not coming back in time for curfew."

"So?" I say. She wouldn't be the first to miss curfew

around here. A lot of the girls couldn't care less about curfew.

"We heard her talking on the phone this morning. I guess her boyfriend has lots of money. And he told her that he bought them a place a few hours away."

I raise my eyebrows in surprise. "Really? Do any of the staff know?"

"No, it sounds like she's just going to leave. But she seemed really excited. She kept telling him how much she loved him and how they'd finally be able to get away from everyone and start their new life together."

It's hard to imagine Trina in a loving relationship with someone with her abrasive attitude. Then again, maybe that's why she's so mad — she can't spend as much time with the person she loves while here at Haywood.

"Hmm …" I say. I can't help but feel a little jealous. How I wish I had a nice boyfriend to run away with. My track record isn't the greatest though. I probably wouldn't even know a nice boy if I met one. That's another similarity between all the girls in this place. We're all so desperate for love that we'll settle for anyone who pays any attention to us, good or bad.

If Trina's found love, she's pretty lucky. It would be awesome to leave here for a life of love with someone. Maybe start a family. Raise my baby in a loving environment where it would never know pain.

I'm waiting for Lisa to make her next move in our game when I see Trina coming down the hallway. She's moving quickly and with purpose, and for once she has a humungous smile on her face. She looks lost in happy thoughts and not her usual sullen self.

Trina has been here for three weeks now, and not one of us has even gotten more than three words out of her. She's kept to herself the entire time, continuing to eat meals on her own too.

"That's good for her," I say, distracted. I know I should be concentrating on the game but I can't stop staring at Trina. Something is definitely up. I watch as she pulls open the door to the sleeping area and disappears from sight.

"Uh, hello, Andy?" Lisa says, waving her hands in front of my face.

"Sorry," I mutter. "Is it okay if we quit now? I'm not into it anymore." I throw my hand of cards down onto the tabletop and push my chair back to get up. Lisa looks at me like I'm crazy and starts picking up the cards.

"Fine," she says, clearly irritated with me.

When I open the doors to the sleeping area, Trina is rolling her clothes and stuffing them in her backpack. She looks up, startled, takes one look at me and continues. I head to my bed and open the book I'm reading. I periodically glance over at her, but she's preoccupied with filling her backpack. What Lisa said must be true. She's packing, all right. I lie there and imagine someone coming for me, to take us to our new life and our new home. I imagine him holding out his arm, eager to lead me to our waiting vehicle. In my daydream I'm like Cinderella, being led to our chariot. But real life isn't like that. I know better. It won't be long before I'll be leaving Haywood, but there's no one waiting for me and I don't have a home to go to.

Sure enough, after supper has ended, Trina bolts out of the cafeteria and then appears just minutes later, her bulging backpack on her shoulders. The girls are whispering about it and staring. There's a dreamy smile on her face and she doesn't realize that the rest of us are watching her.

"Where you off to?" Madge asks, staring at her backpack.

"Out with my boyfriend," I hear Trina say.

"Alright. We'll see you at eleven," Madge says, bidding her goodbye.

We're allowed to go out at night, but curfew is at eleven. If anyone is late, she has to do double the chores the next day and toilet duty. Many of the girls feel it's a small price to pay to have some extra fun. But if you don't come home at all, you essentially get grounded and can't go out for two weeks. You also get put on probation and if it happens again, you lose your place at Haywood. For some, that's not a bad thing. But if your only alternative is the streets, Haywood can start looking pretty good.

I walk to the front foyer where Trina is waiting eagerly by the door, scanning every car for her boyfriend.

"See ya." I wave. Trina turns and looks at me, her face still lit with excitement. She's actually beautiful when she smiles.

"Bye," Trina says and turns back to the doorway. I can practically feel her anticipation. I decide to go back and read, anxious to get lost in something. Trina is off to start a new life and I can't help but feel pangs of envy. I've been here for so many years that it's hard watching others leave. I wonder what the future holds for them.

At ten o'clock, I head back to the front so that I can grab a new book from the bookcases that line the reception area. Almost all of the girls are out. I like staying in on these nights for the privacy. The building is quiet except for the noise coming from the staff sitting at the cafeteria tables. They are visiting and having coffee and their laughter echoes through the building. I jump when I see a figure sitting in one of the chairs. It's Trina, with her backpack still sitting squarely on her shoulders.

She quickly stands and returns to the door, as though nothing is out of the ordinary, but it's been hours that she's been in this room waiting. Not wanting to embarrass her or intrude, I quickly grab another book and head back. I wonder why she's still standing there. Her boyfriend is obviously very late. Maybe he isn't due to come yet. I'd probably stand for hours waiting too, if it were me, on the off chance that he'd come early.

I get ready for bed and put on my coziest pajamas. At eleven, once all the girls have trickled in, Gertie starts shutting off some of the lights to dim the place. Although I've barely read the new book I've grabbed, curiosity gets the best of me and I decide to take it back to the foyer. I put my slippers on to warm my feet from the cold tile floors, knowing full well that my real intention is to see if Trina is gone.

I'm relieved when I get to the foyer and the chairs are empty. There is no one standing in front of the door. I even put my face to the window and shield the glare from the light so that I can see around the yard and the street in the dark. Trina's nowhere to be found.

I imagine her bursting with joy right now, speeding off in her boyfriend's car to start a new life.

Trina is probably giggling uncontrollably, in between kisses from her boyfriend who is driving with one hand, his other wrapped around her protectively. The car is packed with their belongings, her hand resting comfortably on his thigh as they drive, feeling carefree and hopeful.

I feel sorry for myself, imagining Trina's good fortune.

Just as I'm about to head for bed, I hear a soft sob somewhere in the room. I look around but see nothing. "Hello?" I whisper. But there is no response and for a moment, I wonder if I'm imagining things. Then I hear another sob, and another, and another, until there is no mistaking it. I make my way around the room, looking behind the chairs and scanning the corners of the room.

On the next sob, I whirl around to see a dark figure curled up on the floor behind a giant floor plant. Startled, I rush to see who it is. Something in my gut tells me it's Trina even before I see her. And sure enough, when I place my hand on her arms, which she has buried her head into, her tear-stained face meets mine.

"Trina?" I say softly.

She continues to cry, her backpack shaking with every sob. I don't know if I should be here or if I should just go away and leave her alone. To be honest, I am a bit nervous. With her attitude, I wouldn't be surprised if she took a swing at me or told me off. I sit beside her for several minutes without saying a word. I wonder if any of the other girls have seen her here, but then I realize that's unlikely. I would've heard all about it.

"He left without me," Trina says finally. Her voice drips with pain, the pain of broken hearts and broken dreams. "He said he'd come … that he got us a place … that we'd get married," she speaks in broken sentences, still sobbing. "I love him more than anything … and he's gone."

"Maybe he's still coming," I offer. Trina shakes her head, her whole body heaving.

"He called …" She cries. "He said we're done and that he's taking someone else. Some Asha girl he's been cheating on me with." She dissolves into heavy sobs once again. "Oh, Jeremy!"

How could you? I want to say to her boyfriend. *Don't you know what you're taking away here? Our dreams are wrapped up in you, in escape, in a better life. How dare you take that away from girls like us! Girls who have lost everything and have nothing left.* But realistically, if Jeremy's been cheating and decides to run away with another girl, he's probably not her happy ending either. Try telling Trina that though, when her heart is shattered into a thousand pieces.

"Trina, you're too good for him. He doesn't deserve you then," I say as I wrap my arms around her. I don't know Trina at all, so I'm not sure if my statement holds true, but she looks up at me and gives me a tiny smile.

"Why are you being nice to me?" she asks. "I haven't exactly been nice to anyone since I've been here."

"We're all in this together," I say, though I know that's not quite true. "Look, I don't want to see you so hurt. We've all been through so much. None of us are strangers to pain. We gotta stick together if we're going to make it." I rub her back with my hand and she instantly relaxes a bit. We sit there for almost a half hour before we hear Gertie clear her throat. I'm not sure how long she's been in the room. I don't know what she's heard. She's obviously been looking for us.

"Girls?" she says peering at us, as though she's trying to figure out what's going on. "Time for bed."

"We're just going," I say, looking squarely at Gertie to try and let her know that I've got this. We jump to our feet. I slide Trina's backpack off of her and carry it, my other arm wrapped around her waist. She wipes her face with her arms, trying to regain her composure. Gertie watches, she seems pleasantly surprised at our newfound friendship. She smiles and pats me on the back as we pass her.

"Please don't tell anyone," Trina pleads.

"I won't," I promise.

Together we walk through the double doors to our beds. I can already hear the whispers of the girls who are still awake, wondering why Trina is still here. I pull back my covers and turn to look at her, but the only thing I see is a figure heaving under the blankets.

Chapter 8

Fall 2003

It's like I've landed in a whole other life, my past left behind. After a glorious summer spent swimming, camping, and helping Shelley take care of the flowers and vegetable garden in the yard, I feel like I'm in heaven. They've even bought me a bike, a shiny purple mountain bike. Luke taught me how to ride it, and I can go down the street and around the block by myself. I've met a couple of kids from down the street and we run back and forth from our yards playing tag or running through the sprinkler. After two and a half months here, the weather has turned cooler and leaves have started to fall from the trees.

Grade five has started and, for the first time, I'm popular and have lots of friends. Before, I was picked last for teams, whispered about, and snickered at. But here, at St. Philip, no one knows my past. It's like I've created a whole new identity for myself. Girls are clamoring to sit with me, often fawning over a sparkly headband or a new shirt I'm wearing. I've never worn anything that someone else admired. I have beautiful clothes, my hair is in braids or ponytails and it's always clean. My delicious lunches are filled with more food than even I can eat. I finally feel like I don't have to eat everything in sight. I start to realize that I don't have to worry about the next meal. And boy, can Shelley cook. She makes all sorts of delicious meals, often letting me help. She's taught me how to measure ingredients and follow a recipe, and being in the kitchen preparing food thrills me.

Shelley has even made a lifebook for me. It's something all foster children are supposed to have, basically an album of photos, special mementos, and memories that I can keep forever so that I have a history and a sense of where I've come from and what I've done. Debby says that foster parents are supposed to make lifebooks with the children and that once they're made they become the child's property. Even if the child moves from home to home, they can add to their lifebook and keep it with them.

We've collected a whole shoebox of memories so far. Shelley says she wishes she had pictures of me as a baby so that she could add them in. "You must have been a beautiful baby," she assures me. But my mother, Jacqueline, must not have thought so. I don't think I was ever beautiful to her. Shelley says we'll need a crate by the time we're done filling it with memories.

Shelley and Luke have enrolled me in soccer. I don't really like the constant running; my feet betray me often and I trip over myself when trying to control the ball. But even so, I live for the days when our team has a game, because there is nothing like having people there to watch me play. *ME!* My heart leaps whenever I look over to the edge of the field and see Shelley and Luke smiling wide, clapping, and cheering me on. Shelley's hair is lifted by the wind, the sun bouncing off of her golden hair. She is so beautiful she shimmers. I burst with pride knowing that I get to go home with the two of them.

The Thiessens aren't able to have children of their own. That's what Shelley told me. They were hoping to adopt, but they've been on a waiting list for years. They decided to become foster parents and as it turns out, I am their very first foster child.

"I'm so happy you've come to stay with us," Shelley tells me one evening. She is tucking me into bed. We've had a snack and she's just finished a chapter from a book we are reading. She bends forward and kisses me on the forehead before wrapping me in a big, warm hug. I melt into her and kiss her back. She has no idea how much I love being here.

"Will I get to stay here forever?" I ask, knowing that she probably doesn't have the answer. Would they want to keep me? Could I be that lucky?

"I don't know, sweetheart…." Shelley says, and I believe her. She strokes the hair from my forehead and kisses me again.

I haven't seen my mother since I left for school that last day, the day I told everyone about life at home and was taken to the Thiessens'. I know from their conversations that Jacqueline is still on drugs and that she still can't take care of me. But the bigger issue is that Jacqueline doesn't even want to. I can't imagine the thought of going back to live there. I can't imagine saying good-bye to Shelley and Luke, who have been so good to me. I want them to be my mom and dad, my forever family.

"Goodnight, honey," Shelley whispers. She turns out the light and closes the door partway so that I can go to sleep. I hear Luke approach. "Oh, Luke.…" I hear Shelley say. "She's just asked me if she'll be able to stay here forever!" I can see their shadowy figures embracing in the hallway. He holds her close.

"Well … maybe we can make that happen," he says.

I strain to hear what they are saying, but it's tough to make out when Shelley's face is buried in his chest and they are both talking in low voices. "Really?" Shelley says.

"Why not? Her mom isn't doing anything to get her back. She'll probably be a permanent ward soon and we're the most stable home she's ever had. Why can't we apply to adopt her?" he says. "Let's call Debby about it." I wait for Shelley's response, but all I hear are sniffles. She's crying and kissing Luke, excited at the thought of making me hers forever.

I snuggle deep into my covers, my heart soaring. I'm going to be theirs, I just know it. I'm going to be theirs forever.

Chapter 9

The morning after Trina's boyfriend leaves her stranded at Haywood, I sleep in. I only wake when I hear Monica call for me. When I turn over to look at her, she lets out a sigh of relief. "She's still in bed," Monica calls back out the door behind her. The clang of cutlery on the porcelain dishes and the voices of the girls in the dining hall having breakfast fill the space.

"You sick?" she asks me.

"No," I say.

"She's fine," Monica calls back. Everyone must be wondering where I am because I'm usually one of the first ones to head for breakfast.

"I'll be there soon," I say, sitting up in bed.

When the double doors close with a thud, the room becomes quiet again. Thinking I'm alone, I stretch and yawn and let out a sigh. Then I remember the night before and turn to Trina's bed, the one that used to be Mandy's. Trina is awake, lying on her back staring at the ceiling. I glance at her arms, which are stretched out beside her. I spot cuts in various lengths across her arms and realize that the cuts are fresh, most likely something she's done during the night.

"I used to do that too," I say, pointing to her arms. Trina stiffens and covers her arms with the blanket. "Got the marks to prove it," I tell her, extending my arms out for her to see. Even when you get healthier, you never forget. I have scars that will stay with me forever.

Trina looks surprised, as though she's never met anyone who has done it before. I think of the help I got to stop. Perhaps Betty can help Trina too.

"I haven't done it in a really long time," I explain. "Betty helped me stop."

Trina pushes the blanket down and lifts her arms up to inspect them. She looks sad as she runs the tips of her fingers up each of her forearms. Trina looks back at my arms thoughtfully, as though she's never considered that there may be a way to stop.

"C'mon. Let's go get breakfast," I say to her, springing up from my bed. I go to her and offer her a hand up. She looks at me for a moment, unsure, and then takes my hand, following me towards the dining hall.

When the other girls catch sight of the two of us approaching hand-in-hand, the activity in the room seems to stop.

"What's wrong, did Prince Charming get lost?" Analise snickers. Laughter follows from a few of the other girls.

"Yeah, thought you were out of here," Monica says. Everyone stares at Trina, waiting for an answer. I can see Trina's fists balling up, tears filling her eyes again. Her teeth clench. I know she doesn't need to be provoked.

"Lay off," I tell them firmly. Monica and Analise look at me in surprise. "She's one of us. Cut the crap."

I lead Trina to the buffet table to get our meal, knowing full well that all eyes are on us. Trina smiles gratefully at me once the rest of the girls shuffle out of the room.

"Thanks, Andy," she says. "For everything."

It isn't long before Trina is sitting with us at mealtimes and joining in our activities. She's pretty quiet and doesn't really share with the others, but I'm glad she's opening up to me at least. As we get to know each other, even Trina's look is changing. Her look has softened as she lets her guard down. She has toned down the heavy eyeliner and is letting her hair grow out. It's like she's dropped the tough girl persona a bit.

At Haywood, once you turn sixteen it is mandatory to start taking the 'Life Skills' program. Basically it means that the older girls have to start doing some of the shopping and cleaning. We have to make a meal plan and work together to make a meal a couple of times a week. Betty gives us the money to go and get the things we need. Haywood even supplies a car for us to use, provided we have our license, as long as we have a staff member with us for supervision.

Trina and I have been working together closely. She knows nothing in the kitchen. It's a room with foreign tools to her. Because I used to cook with Shelley, I know my way around a kitchen pretty well and I'm teaching Trina what I know.

Today we are cooking chicken lasagna for supper. I'm sautéing onions and pieces of chicken breasts while Trina grates mozzarella cheese. The smell of the meat cooking makes my mouth water.

"Are you going to be able to hold yourself back, Andy?" Trina says, laughing. "You look like you're about to dig in!"

I smile. I admit that waiting for the meal is my biggest challenge. I reach over and scoop some mozzarella cheese from the cutting board, popping it in my mouth before Trina can say anything. Being around food just doesn't get old for me.

"My mom never bought cheese," Trina says softly. The remark seems to have come out of nowhere. She's staring intently at the pile of cheese.

"Mine neither," I say.

"It was always too expensive. At least that's what she said," Trina recalls. Although we're only talking about cheese, I can tell by the look on her face that we're really talking about so much more. "There are a lot of things she didn't buy. She really wasn't good at taking care of my sister and me."

"You have a sister?"

"Karissa. She was four years younger than me." Trina swallows and pauses. "She was the cutest little girl. I adored her. I think I was more the parent than my mom was."

I nod, unsure of how to respond. Trina doesn't usually share a lot.

"When we got taken away, Karissa and I were separated. At first I got to see her every few weeks. The social worker would bring her over for visits. I couldn't wait to see her each time. She looked good. Healthy. Her foster family seemed to take good care of her. When it started to feel like it was too long since we had last seen each other, I started asking about her, but no one would tell me anything. Then one day the social worker showed up. She told me my sister had drowned in a swimming pool." Trina sucks in a deep breath. "I never got to say good-bye."

I set down my utensil and put my arms around Trina. She stiffens a bit, then relaxes. "I'm sorry, Trina," I whisper.

I've never had a sister, but I definitely know what loss feels like.

"I was never the same after that," Trina says.

We stand hugging for a moment, and then go back to preparing the meal. We work in silence, thinking of our pasts.

"I'm going to buy tons of cheese when I'm outta here," Trina says suddenly. I look at her and then we both burst out laughing.

Later, the two of us talk long into the night. It turns out that Trina didn't have much of a home life with her mother either. Trina's mom, Lucy, had become unexpectedly pregnant with her too, but at age fifteen. Lucy had grown up in poverty herself, so she didn't know any other life. She hadn't been ready for parenthood. Because she was so young, her friends were out partying and having a good time. Lucy didn't want to miss out so she left Trina alone for long periods of time so that she could go out with her friends. A neighbour called the police after realizing that Trina and her little sister had been left alone in the apartment for two straight days, and the girls were put in foster care.

Trina's been in ten foster homes in ten years. She's even been in juvie a few times. She's got quite the rap sheet. She's been charged with theft, assault, trespassing, carrying a weapon, and a few failures to appear in court. Her quest to have someone, anyone, care about her has put her in a whole mess of toxic relationships, mostly with guys who show the slightest interest in her, but who are all terribly wrong for her. She's begged, borrowed, and stolen for almost every guy she's dated. She's even taken the rap for them, keeping them out of jail by confessing to the police that she'd done it all and they'd had no part.

Caseworkers and various police officers have all tried to reason with her and get her back on the straight and narrow. "This isn't the right path for you, Trina," they'd say, knowing full well that although Trina's childhood hasn't been the best, the guys in her life had been orchestrating the criminal activity all along. But Trina is loyal, and the caseworkers and the cops aren't the ones holding her at night, telling her how beautiful and tough she is, making her heart swell with pride. Her boyfriend Jeremy was doing that, and if ripping off an old lady in the street or robbing a convenience store was what it took to hear those words, she'd do it.

"We've got a new placement for you. It is part of your conditions," her caseworker had told her shortly after her release from the last thirty day sentence. Where? How far away? The thought of leaving Jeremy for any length of time would be unbearable. But Jeremy assured her he'd get her out quickly so that they could build a life together.

"They've got a spot for you at Haywood."

Chapter 10

September 2003

"Bernice, honey, where are you?" Shelley calls. I am sitting against the big oak tree in the backyard with a notebook and a pen. I am writing a story. I've been writing a lot lately. My teacher keeps encouraging me to write. He says I have a great use of language and vivid imagery. He tells me that I have a gift and that I should continue to develop it. I'm discovering how much I love to write. Just like reading, I can escape for a while and get lost in the page. Luke has even bought me a pink spiral notebook to support and encourage me. I've been writing in it diligently every day.

I am writing about a young girl who is very sick. Her parents love her with all of their hearts and they are determined to save her. I already know how it's going to end. Although her situation seems dire, in the end she's going to make it.

"I'm here," I yell back at Shelley. I peer at her from around the tree and she smiles and waves, satisfied now that she knows where I am. I return to my page with my thoughts tumbling one after another, my pen moving furiously to capture it all. "Just like me, you're going to get a happy ending," I tell my character. "You'll think that it's all over for you and then a miracle happens to change everything."

I smile as I continue writing. I feel powerful wielding this pen, weaving this story. I can decide the fate of my characters with the scrawl of my hand. Great things can happen when you least expect them.

I've been here for about a year and a half now. Shelley and Luke are trying to adopt me. It's a long, drawn-out process and it could take several months, but we're going to be a forever family. I have my miracle.

Mrs. Assaly, our elderly next door neighbour, is watering her garden. She still does all of her yardwork herself. She glances over at me and smiles approvingly. "I used to love to draw when I was your age," she says. "I'd sit under a tree just like that and draw for hours." I give her a polite smile and return to my notebook. "Good for you, dear. You keep that up!" she says to me.

"Do you still draw, Mrs. Assaly?" I ask.

She shakes her head sadly. "No. I'm afraid I don't," she says. She looks down at her garden for a few minutes before speaking again. "I stopped drawing after my Henry died," she says, referring to her husband who passed away five years earlier.

I nod with understanding. "Well, if it made you feel so good, maybe you should start drawing again," I offer. After all, why give up something that fills your heart with joy?

Mrs. Assaly smiles at me and nods. "You know, my dear Bernice," she shakes her head in disbelief at me and then breaks into a chuckle. "I think you may be right."

I hear the backdoor swing open again. "Bernice, I have to pick up Luke and run to the store to get some things for supper," Shelley calls out. "Grab a coat and let's go." Luke woke up to find a flat tire on his car this morning and since we were already running late, Shelley decided to drive him to work in her car rather than have him spend the time changing it. The commute to his work takes about forty-five minutes and I'm not particularly thrilled with abandoning my story to sit in a car during rush hour traffic. I groan at Shelley in disappointment.

"Okay," I say reluctantly.

I snap the notebook shut and start to get up when Mrs. Assaly calls over to Shelley. "If Bernice wants to stay here and write, I don't mind watching her." Mrs. Assaly looks back at me and gives me a sly smile, knowing that I want so desperately to work on my story. I nod in approval, hoping that Shelley agrees.

"That's fine with me if that's what you'd prefer, Bernice. And if you don't mind too much, Mrs. Assaly." I pump my fist in victory and tear open my notebook again. Mrs. Assaly laughs and waves Shelley on.

"Go ahead! She'll be fine. It's no trouble at all." Mrs. Assaly gives me a wink and resumes her watering. Shelley makes her way over to me and plants a kiss on my forehead. Her familiar fruity scent fills the air around me. How I love the way she smells.

"Are you sure you don't want to come?" she asks.

"I'm sure," I tell her. She stands and ruffles my hair with her hand before starting for the door again.

"Thanks, Mrs. Assaly! We won't be too long."

I return to my story, realizing that I'm reaching a pivotal moment. The girl is close to death and if the doctors don't do something soon, she could die. They suggest an experimental treatment that is extremely risky, but her parents must decide the course of action immediately. Knowing that they'll lose their daughter if they don't try this new treatment, they give their consent to the doctors to go ahead. They want their daughter to have the best chance at survival so that she can go on to live a happy, productive life. She's been through so much already, having suffered horribly from her illness. Her parents know that their decision could be the key to her survival, that they alone can make the choice to save her.

I write furiously, barely looking up from my notebook. Mrs. Assaly calls over and asks if I want something to eat. "That's okay, Mrs. Assaly. I'll wait for Luke and Shelley to get home," I reply. Mrs. Assaly is a great cook, but mealtimes with Luke and Shelley are my favourite. We sit around the table, clasp our hands, and say a prayer. The table is always set so nicely, the platters of steaming food artfully arranged. Shelley always makes more than enough food. She laughs at how I can't seem to get enough, how I still rave about her cooking at each meal. "You are my number one fan, Bernice," she laughs. During the meal, I love how they ask me about my day, how they seem so genuinely interested. I feel so safe and cared for. We've turned into a real family.

I write until my hand starts to get sore. By now the sun has set and the air has gotten cooler. I rub my arms vigorously with my hands, hoping to warm my skin. My stomach is growling and I realize that I'm hungrier than

I thought. I stand up and brush the fallen leaves and dirt from my pants. Mrs. Assaly is sitting on her patio with a cup of tea and what looks like an album.

"May I come over?" I ask her. She waves me over. I push myself up in the air and over the fence and land with a thump on her side of the yard. She chuckles while I pick myself off of the ground. "Sorry ... I guess I should have used the gate," I say sheepishly.

"I would have done the same thing at your age." Mrs. Assaly laughs. I take a seat beside her at the patio table.

"Whatcha doing?" I ask. Mrs. Assaly rubs the front of the album she's holding, a forlorn smile on her face.

"You were right, Bernice," she says, opening the album. Expecting to see photographs, my eyes light up in surprise when I see that the album contains dozens of drawings carefully posted on the pages.

"Are these yours?" I ask. Mrs. Assaly places the album in front of me so that I can have a better look. I carefully turn the pages, staring at the gorgeous images. Most of them are of people of all ages and sizes. The people look so real, it's hard to imagine that they were drawn.

Mrs. Assaly smiles nervously. "It's been quite a few years since I've last looked at these," she admits.

"Oh, Mrs. Assaly, you must continue drawing! These are incredible!" I breathe. How could someone with so much talent give this up? Mrs. Assaly looks closely at me before reaching for the album.

"You may have changed my mind, Bernice. I think you've inspired me." She flips through the pages herself, lost in thought. My heart swells with pride knowing that Mrs. Assaly may draw again and that I had something to do with it. If she's as passionate about drawing as I am about writing, how in the world could she possibly give it up?

The wind starts to pick up and the leaves start to lift and swirl above the ground. It's starting to get dark. Although Mrs. Assaly and I are having a wonderful time together, I'm anxious for Luke and Shelley to get back. They'll be so excited to hear about Mrs. Assaly and her drawings. When the pages of her album keep getting blown open by the wind, Mrs. Assaly suggests we go inside the house and wait. I help her stack the patio chairs and carry in the album for her. We sit in front of the TV and she brings me some cookies and milk. "I'm sure you're hungry dear," she says. "It might be awhile before you have dinner." I am thankful for the snack. The growling in my stomach is getting louder and it's starting to make me anxious. Feeling this hungry brings back too many memories. It's as though the emptiness of my stomach has paralleled the emptiness inside my heart throughout the years. *But it's different now*, I try to assure myself. *You have a loving family, a safe home, and lots of food to eat. It'll be okay and you'll eat soon.*

Mrs. Assaly keeps glancing at the clock, watching vigilantly out the window every time she sees a pair of headlights making their way down the street, to see if it is Luke and Shelley. I'm focusing on the game show on TV. Adults are playing against children to see who is smarter. I'm amused by this show, how the kids are clearly smarter than the adults. Many of the answers come easily to me and I laugh when I see the adults scratching their heads, asking for help.

At last, a pair of headlights turns into Luke and Shelley's driveway. Mrs. Assaly breathes a sigh of relief.

"They're home!" she says brightly. I get up from the couch and stretch, grateful to be going home now. Mrs. Assaly walks to the front door and pulls it open. She hesitates at the doorway and puts her hand over her mouth.

"Stay here," she advises me. Immediately, my heart starts to beat faster. *What's going on?* I wonder. I make my way towards the door but when I look outside, it's not Luke and Shelley at all. It's a man in a police uniform, walking towards Luke and Shelley's doorway and he's clutching his hat in his hands.

I watch as Mrs. Assaly dashes down the steps towards him. I stand at the top of her front steps, watching, my feet frozen in place. The officer looks at Mrs. Assaly and then up to me before clearing his throat uncomfortably. Mrs. Assaly cups her hand over her mouth, horror in her eyes, and somehow before anything is said, I know.

In seconds, I vaguely hear Mrs. Assaly talking to me. She is wrapping her arms around me, as though shielding me from the news. I can hear the police officer speaking in low tones, but I don't make out what he is saying. Instead my mind is thinking of the girl in my story, the one who is very ill. I think of her lying in that hospital bed while her parents talk to the doctor.

"We've made our decision," they say. "We've decided against the experimental treatment. It's time for us to let her go." The doctor nods in understanding. And with that, the parents walk hand in hand out of the hospital while their daughter gasps in horror, knowing that her fate has been sealed. There will be no miracle for her, no happy ending. She won't be saved after all.

Chapter 11

I am sitting in a conference room in Haywood with Betty, my new caseworker Sharon, and other officials from social services responsible for my welfare, but I'm not sure who they are exactly. They are here to discuss my upcoming departure from Haywood. I will be eighteen in April, which is just one month away and that means I can no longer stay here. I've known that this time would come, but I'm still quite nervous.

I want to believe that I have the courage to face the real world and that I can make it on my own, yet I wonder how I'm going to handle it all. The caseworker has designed a plan for me, which includes securing my own apartment. Social services will pay my rent until I'm done school. They've asked what my future plans are. *Survival*, I want to say. But that's not the answer they are looking for.

As we move out on our own, we are supposed to have goals, dreams, and things to aspire to. I find it hard to imagine how I'm supposed to dream when I'm constantly worried about how I'm going to manage to eat, sleep, and keep a roof over my head. Our dreams are different from other kids our age. We don't expect as much from life as other kids do because our dreams were robbed from us long ago.

"You are almost done high school, Andy. That's a huge accomplishment." Sharon says to me. All of the people at the table nod in agreement. "Have you thought about furthering your education? Your marks are very good." I shrug. Sure I've thought about school, but how will I make it all work? At Haywood, almost everything is provided for us. We can focus on our studies. But when I get out into the world on my own, how will I do it? I'm going to have so much more to worry about.

So many girls my age can't wait to get out on their own. They are counting the days until they leave home, anxious to have their own place and a space of their own. Take Trina for example. She can't wait to leave Haywood. She tried to have herself discontinued from foster care when she turned sixteen. But after an exhaustive search, no one could be found to assume guardianship of her. No matter how hard they tried, the caseworkers couldn't find extended family or close friends who might want to take her in. Trina told me how much it hurt, knowing that her mother or grandmother wouldn't have anything to do with her even though she'd expected that they'd feel that way. What hurt even more was that there wasn't even one significant relationship in her life that the caseworker could consider for placement. In the entire world, when it came down to it, Trina only had herself. We are so much more alike than I imagined. *Throwaway girls*, I like to call us.

I've discovered that Haywood is also the clos-est thing to a support system I've had for a long time.

When I'm on my own, who can I go to? My caseworker, Sharon, keeps telling me that I can contact her anytime, but I only see her every few months. She barely knows me. Somehow knowing that watching out for me is one of her job requirements, I have a hard time imagining us getting close. And that's the other problem. Caseworkers change every five seconds, which means that there really isn't an opportunity to get close to any of them. Don't get me wrong, they've all been really nice to me over the years. It's not their fault the system is the way it is.

We've had two meetings so far about my exit from Haywood. I know that the next meeting will be my last. Because I don't know what my future goals may be at this time, I tell them that I want to focus on working for now. "Deadlines for applications for post-secondary education are approaching," Sharon reminds me. "I'd hate for you to miss out on starting in the fall because your application didn't make it in on time."

I shift uncomfortably in my seat. I know I should feel like the world is opening up to me, that I have so many choices for my future. But the thing is, I've never given the future much thought. How can I envision the future when I am trying to get through the present? Social services will pay for my apartment and my education until I'm twenty-one, as long as I'm going to school and working part of the time to help pay my expenses. I know there are kids that would die for this opportunity, but it's just all so overwhelming to me. The women around the table are all looking at me expectantly. "I'll give it some more thought," I say.

One of the women slides a package of brochures and information sheets from various post-secondary institutions. "These may help," she says. I nod and add them to the sheets I've already been given.

"Well, it looks like you're almost ready," Sharon says, smiling. The women start to rise from their seats. I smile halfheartedly at them and gather my information.

Betty gives me a supportive squeeze when we get to the doorway of the conference room. "I guess we'll both be leaving here soon, won't we?" she says. She has recently announced her retirement and will be leaving just weeks after me. I nod and feel tears well up. Betty has a whole family to be with. She's already planning to watch a few of her grandchildren part time after her retirement from Haywood. She'll be surrounded by those she loves.

I make my way back to the sleeping area. Trina is standing in the hallway waiting for me and she lights up when she sees me. "So, how did it go?" she says excitedly. "When are you officially outta here?" Trina turns eighteen a month after me and she's determined that we're going to live together once it's her turn to leave.

"I move into the apartment on June fifteenth," I tell her. She squeals with delight and claps her hands.

"It's going to be so great getting out of here," she says. "Just wait until I get out and we're living together … then it'll really be awesome!" She's chattering non-stop, detailing all the things we're going to do. I'm only half listening though. I'm trying to think of what my goals should be and whether I should even apply for school. What would I take? What have I wanted to be?

I feel like I've been kicked in the stomach. There's only one thing I ever thought of doing with my life. It was something I loved, but gave up years ago: Writing. It was my escape. It allowed to me to dream up things I couldn't see otherwise. It gave me hope. It filled me with such satisfaction that I could think of doing nothing else.

Grief washes over me as I recall the last time I wrote anything. How I had convinced Mrs. Assaly to start drawing again because I couldn't imagine how she could have stopped in the first place. Then came the long, fateful night when my whole world was shattered. Luke and Shelley never came home. And then I understood exactly why Mrs. Assaly had put down her pen once her husband died. Loss has a way of robbing us of more than just the people we love. I know this because I've never written since.

"Andy, are you listening?" Irina says, turning to me. "Andy, what's wrong?" she says, clearly stunned by the look on my face. "Why are you crying?" Tears fall uncontrollably down my face. Writing. It's the only thing I ever wanted to do. But I have no idea if I can ever bring myself to do it again.

Chapter 12

November 2003

I feel dead. I am a walking zombie, numb all the way through. In a flash, I have lost everything. Maybe it's easier to never have loved after all, and then you can't feel the pain of having lost it.

Larry and Sandra Puhler are my new foster parents. I am in a tiny house in a dilapidated part of town, not too far from where I remember living with my mother. Including me, there are three foster kids here, and we all share a room. There are two sets of bunk beds in our tiny bedroom. They take up so much space that our clothes have to be kept in the closet because there is no room for a dresser. Larry and Sandra also have three kids of their own. Two of them are babies and they sleep in the basement with Larry and Sandra while the other one, who is six, has her own room beside ours. The house is packed to the brim with furniture and various knick-knacks. Larry's penchant for junk, or what he thinks is collecting, has filled this house to capacity. The house has a hot plate, a microwave, and a small refrigerator. The stove is sitting broken in the corner of the kitchen. There are no elaborate dinners being made in this house, simply ready-to-eat meals that can be stirred in a pot or warmed in the microwave. There is no dining table to speak of. We just eat wherever a seat can be found. It's such a far cry from my life with Luke and Shelley that it makes the pain of losing them that much worse.

Larry and Sandra are nice enough, I guess. I mean they don't really talk much to the kids. Larry is out of work a lot of the time, taking odd jobs here and there. Groceries are a big deal here, and food leaves the house just as quickly as it comes in. For once in my life, I don't care about food. Whenever it's time to eat, all I can think of is Shelley cooking in her beautiful kitchen and the love that went into those meals. I can't bring myself to put much into my mouth. When I do, it's tasteless.

My new school is a joke. I don't even pay attention half the time. I don't understand what the point is. What do I care about science and math? Long division is a waste of my time. Something divided by something always leaves you a little something or nothing at all. Isn't that all I need to know?

Many of my classmates are in the same boat as me. They couldn't care less about learning, so I fit right in. Sometimes we cut class by leaving during afternoon recess. No one calls home to tell our parents. It's like it's considered a bonus if we show up at all. Once upon a time I would have felt guilty for cutting class and slacking off in school. I can only imagine how Luke and Shelley would have reacted if I'd done this sort of thing at my old school. I could never have done that to them though. I was so desperate for their love and approval; I would have died if they had shown any disappointment in me.

It's a funny thing when no one is looking for you. You can disappear for hours at a time and have no one to answer to, which is good because I'm in no mood to answer to anybody. If anything, I want someone to answer to me for once and tell me why the only people I've ever truly loved have been taken from me forever. But no one discusses this with me. No one has the answers.

The two other foster children who live with me are both twelve. They are twins whose names are Hunter and Stephanie. They've been with the Puhlers for about six months. They don't mind it here because they are free to do as they please. Both of them skip school all the time and spend hours away from the house. At first I barely noticed because I was grateful for the privacy.

"Wanna come with us?" Stephanie asks me one night. Everyone has just finished eating macaroni and cheese and once again I've skipped the meal to stay in my room. "We're heading out for a bit," she says. Stephanie has long brown hair that she pulls into a ponytail and teases until it's full and fluffy. She's a pretty girl, but she wears a ton of makeup day and night. It's so thick it looks like a mask and when I look at her I want to scrape it off just to see what she looks like underneath. Hunter is waiting outside our bedroom window. Curiosity about how they spend their time gets the best of me, and I nod and jump down from my bed. Stephanie smiles and takes me by the hand. Hunter's face registers surprise when he sees me following Stephanie but he quickly smiles.

"Cool," he says. "Let's go."

I walk with them, unsure of our destination. It's already dark. Being that it is late fall there is a definite chill in the air. Winter is fast approaching. The streets are pretty quiet except for a few clusters of kids. Most of them are our age or teenagers. Some of them look tough and walk with a swagger. Some of them seem to be looking for someone to stare down. But I'm not intimidated. There's nothing that anyone can do to me that will hurt more than what I've just been through. *Try your best*, I think. *You got nothing*.

Stephanie and Hunter are talking amongst themselves, swearing and spitting as they walk. Stephanie pulls a pack of cigarettes from her jacket pocket and turns to offer me one. I've never smoked before. I shake my head no and jam my hands in my pockets. She shrugs and lights one up. The smoke blows into my face, stinging my eyes and nostrils. I can't even stand the smell, let alone how they might taste.

Just as we're about to round the corner, another group of teens appear and make their way towards us. Stephanie nudges Hunter and our walking slows.

"Hunter!" the tall one of the group calls. Hunter waves at him and makes his way towards him.

"Wassup?" Hunter says. They do some kind of hand-shake and bump shoulders.

"Just chillin," the tall one says. He's talking to Hunter but staring at me. "Who's this?" he says.

"Aw, that's Bernice," Stephanie says. "She's livin' with us."

He takes a walk around me and runs his finger down my arm. "Welcome," he says admiringly. I flinch at his touch and shoot him a dirty look. "A feisty one," he says. The others laugh.

"She's cool, Marcus," Stephanie says. She narrows her eyes at him and gives Hunter a look for them to move along. Hunter clears his throat.

"See you around," he says, nodding at Marcus and his crew. They all nod back and we continue down the sidewalk. Stephanie immediately starts talking.

"That's Marcus. He's a big deal around here. He's running a lot of stuff on the streets," Stephanie whispers. I have no idea what she means exactly, but I know enough to figure out that Marcus is someone who is used to being respected.

"Isn't he hot?" She gushes. It wasn't exactly easy to make out his features in the dark, so I really don't have a good idea of what he looks like. I just know that when he touched me, I had the urge to reach out and break his finger. Something about the way he did it made my stomach coil.

Hunter stops walking and turns to us. "Stay here," he instructs. Stephanie pulls me to the side of a building and we sink down to the ground to sit. I watch as Hunter makes his way to the front of the building. We're at the liquor store. Hunter talks to a few different men as they come in and out of the building and before long he is putting a wad of bills in someone's hands and being handed a brown paper bag.

Looking victorious, Hunter races over to us and high-fives Stephanie. I watch as they unscrew the lid and take turns drinking out of the bottle.

"Here ... have some," Hunter offers. He hands me the bottle. I tilt it up to my mouth, unsure of what I'll taste. The liquid pours fast and furious into my mouth.

It burns my throat and makes my eyes water. I choke a bit and purse my lips to keep from spitting it out. Both Hunter and Stephanie laugh as I attempt to swallow it all.

"First time?" Hunter asks. I nod, wiping my mouth with the back of my hand. All at once my mouth is hot and tingly. I start to feel lightheaded. Hunter takes the bottle from me and pushes back the paper bag to take a sip, but I grab it from him for another swig.

"Ooh, she likes it." Hunter laughs and Stephanie claps and congratulates me.

"Aww, we've broken another one in," she says to Hunter and they both nod in approval. We start to walk back in the direction we came, but this time everything seems out of focus. I love the way my body feels so warm and numb. Hunter and Stephanie pass the bottle back and forth to each other a few times before passing it back to me. By the time we reach the park, I can barely make out where I'm going.

Stephanie smiles and helps me onto a bench. "You'll have to hang with us more often."

My thoughts are racing, but there's no rhyme or reason to what's going on in my head. It's hard to even formulate words to speak. I hear Hunter talking to someone, but I can't make out who it is in the dark until I see a tall shadowy figure. It's that Marcus guy again. He's laughing at something Hunter is saying. A few of the other people in his group join the conversation.

I lean my head back on the top of the bench so that I'm staring straight up at the sky.

"Nice view, isn't it?" I hear, and when I turn my head Marcus is sitting beside me, his head tilted towards the sky.

"There's stars," I say, though it comes out a little slurred. I keep staring at the sky, only glancing at Marcus every minute or so. He's looking at me intently, uninterested in the sky. I fidget a bit, uncomfortable with the attention. Despite the chilly breeze that dances across my face, I have a strong urge to go to sleep. I feel warm fingers on my cheek and realize that they belong to Marcus, who is bent over me, stroking my skin. All at once I feel a combination of alarm and a pleasant flutter in my belly. Instead of wanting to hit him, I feel pleasure. No one has ever touched me like this before.

"Marcus," I hear Hunter say. He is standing over the two of us, but he doesn't look impressed. Marcus laughs again and sits up.

"Relax," he tells Hunter, but I can tell from the tone of Hunter's voice that he isn't happy at all. "We'll see you around," Marcus whispers to me, his breath welcome warmth on my face. He winks and stands up, brushes by Hunter and laughs again.

The feel of his fingers on my face and the thrill it has given me lingers. *Why is he interested in me?* I wonder. Hunter sees the look on my face and hands me the bottle of liquor, but it's almost empty.

"Finish it off," he says. I pull the bottle from the bag and let the burning liquid coat my throat. I wince as I swallow but the warm sensation envelopes me. I realize that all the pain I've been feeling is gone. There are no tears, no feelings of sadness, and no memories tugging at my heart. For the first time in forever, I feel nothing. And feeling nothing at all feels great.

Chapter 13

I've done it. I've applied for university. I've looked over all the brochures and decided to give school a try. If I'm smart and I do well in school, then why shouldn't I try it? I've decided on Arts and Science with a possible major in English. I'm not sure why, but I feel like I'm taking a leap of faith. Somehow I'll be able to make school work while I'm living on my own. Somehow I'll be able to study the written word and pick up a pen again. I don't know how exactly, but I'm going to do it or die trying.

Something has lit a fire under me these days. I know I'm an example to the other girls and I want to make them proud. Knowing I'm leaving soon and knowing how happy everyone is for me and how they'll miss me, maybe I have more of a family here than I thought. It's not perfect, but there is truth to what I told Trina. We do have to look out for each other; we're all we have.

My apartment has been secured. It's a tiny one bedroom in a rougher part of town, but it's affordable and vacant, two requirements that are hard to fulfill in this city these days. There will be basic household furniture and kitchen items already there. I'll even have an allowance aside from my grocery budget to buy some linens and toiletries and other things I will need. I have to admit that as terrified as I am, I'm starting to get excited.

Trina is way more excited than I am. She thinks I'm so lucky that I'll have the freedom to do as I please with no one to answer to. I don't mind having rules in place; it makes me feel like someone is looking out for me, like someone cares. Knowing that Trina will be joining me soon comforts me. We'll have each other.

I've even got a job. I'll be working at McDonald's. It's not much, but the hours are flexible and the manager has assured me that I can take time off when I need to so that I can focus on school. I figure I can also eat meals pretty cheaply most of the time. It might not be that healthy, but at least I won't have to worry about food. The restaurant is just a couple of blocks from the apartment I'll be living in, so I won't have to worry about how I'll get to work and back. It'll be pretty cool to earn a paycheque. I've never been able to do that before. I hope I like it. I hope I can learn it all and be a good employee.

Today is my eighteenth birthday. It's hard to imagine that I'm supposed to be an adult now. I feel so conflicted about age. It feels like I've had to be an adult for so long and yet it also feels like I never really got to be a kid. It's weird to reach this age and have someone officially declare you an adult. If everyone's experiences are so different, how could we all feel the same way at eighteen?

Everyone is lining up in the dining room to sing to me. Betty glides towards me holding a birthday cake, lit with nineteen candles. The room breaks into song, everyone is smiling and clapping. I gaze around the room, grateful for everyone in it. I look at each person's face and see the love in their eyes.

"Nineteen candles. One for each year of your life and an extra for good luck," Betty says, winking at me. I take a deep breath and blow out the candles, secretly hoping for a couple to remain lit. When all are extinguished but one, the room breaks out into raucous laughter.

"Ooh, Andy has a boyfriend," Sheena sings. My cheeks flare with embarrassment but I laugh anyhow.

"We also got you something. Sort of a birthday/going away present," Gertie says. She steps forward with a rectangular shaped package, wrapped in coloured foil and sparkly ribbon. The staff members blink back tears, but Betty's tears flow freely and she keeps staring at the ground, wiping her nose with a tissue. The room is quiet as I open the package. I tear off one end and start on the next.

It's a picture frame. I turn it around so that I can see the front of it and when I do, I feel tears pricking my eyes too. It's a picture of all of us, the girls and the staff at Haywood, taken on the grounds last December. Even Trina is in the picture. It is signed by everyone and in the bottom corner it reads: "To new beginnings … from your family at Haywood."

"We thought you could hang it in your new place," Gertie explains. I hold it close to my body and say thank-you, but the words come out garbled. I start crying uncontrollably, out of love and gratitude and fear and before I know it, everyone has their arms around me, consoling me.

"It's going to be okay, girl," I hear Betty whisper to me. I breathe in the scent of everyone and relish the physical contact. I have to believe that it's going to be okay. I just have to.

Chapter 14

January 2005

It's January. I've been at Larry and Sandra Puhler's house for a little over three months now. It doesn't feel like home. I'm not sure it ever will. I've been spending my days with Hunter, Stephanie, and other kids in the neighbourhood. I attend school most mornings, but by afternoon you'll usually find me sitting in the ditch alongside the train tracks. It's our meeting spot and some days there are a dozen of us passing the time there. Hunter's always bringing bottles of liquor. Mostly I drink enough just to feel a buzz, but if I'm being honest here, there's been a few times that drinking takes the pain away.

It's a cold, blustery winter in the Prairies, so we're often drinking to stay warm. There isn't really any other place for us to go. Most of the kids have parents who are drunk or high all of the time, or there are so many people living in their house that adding extra bodies wouldn't be possible. Larry and Sandra are usually home, and while there really aren't any rules with them, somehow we know that drinking the afternoons away in their tiny bungalow wouldn't be on the list of acceptable practices.

Today is especially windy. I'm wearing a thin hoodie instead of a winter jacket and my body is trembling. None of us are dressed for winter, but not for lack of winter gear. It's more because we think we're too cool to be all bundled up like little kids. Stephanie is cuddled into her new boyfriend, and Hunter is smoking a joint and staring up at the sky.

I'm feeling nervous because Marcus is also with us today. He keeps looking over at me and smiling, making my stomach jump with anxiety. I'm wrapping my arms around my knees, my bottom feeling numb and nearly frozen from sitting in the snow.

"Hey girl," Marcus says, plopping down in the snow beside me. His breath is making warm circles in the air. I turn my head towards him with a shy smile.

"You cold?" he asks. I'm shivering uncontrollably, though I'm not sure it's just the cold. He puts his arm around me protectively and squeezes me close to him. The butterflies in my stomach flutter together furiously. A nervous laugh escapes me and Marcus rubs his hands up and down my arms.

"Come here, I got you," he says, his voice husky and warm. I like having his arms around me. I like being held, it feels comfortable and soothing. The trembling eases and Marcus moves his arm to brush hair from my face and run his fingers down my cheeks again. I feel the same rush of pleasure that I felt the first night in the park. I snuggle deeper into his chest and close my eyes. His smell is a mixture of cologne and cigarettes, but it's pleasant enough that I breathe him in deeply.

The others nod over to each other and stare at us. Some of them are wide-eyed while others are smirking and elbowing each other. I just smile back at them. So what if Marcus is older? So what if he's into me? *Maybe some of them are jealous,* I think. Stephanie gives me a thumbs-up and nudges Hunter, but Hunter isn't impressed. Marcus brushes his lips on my forehead and the heat of his kiss send shivers down my spine. He puts his arm out to one of the guys who quickly hands him the bottle of vodka. Marcus passes it to me and I take a long sip. I hand it to him and he smiles, chugging the clear liquid for several seconds before handing it back.

"That's better," he says. He tips my chin up and kisses me full on the mouth, soft at first, then with more force. There is longing in his kiss and I almost melt in his arms.

"Aw, come on," Hunter grumbles.

Marcus pulls away from me. A white squad car is coasting down the street several metres from our spot. Everybody stiffens, waiting to see if the car is going to stop.

"Gotta jet, beautiful," Marcus says, moving away from me. He jumps to his feet and walks away, gaining speed with each step. I watch as the squad car makes a U-turn to head in the same direction as Marcus. He looks over his shoulder and realizes that the police are following him. The rest of us watch, quiet, and when Marcus disappears from view and the squad car turns down another road, we all breathe a sigh of relief.

I sit in the snow, warmed by the memory of Marcus's touch. It isn't long before Stephanie and Hunter are both high and drunk, but it's starting to get dark and I nudge them for us to leave. I help pull them from the cozy seats they've imprinted in the snow. Everyone waves and we walk home.

When we arrive at the house, Larry and Sandra are glued to the TV. "American Idol" is on and they never miss it. Sandra feels that her true calling is to be a famous rock star, but she has a terrible nasal voice which only worsens when she sings. She's singing along with the contestant at the top of her lungs and the two of them don't even notice that we've come in. There is a box of Pizza Pops open on the counter, empty wrappers across the floor and the sink. Hunter races to the box, eager to have something to eat.

The view of the TV is obstructed from the kitchen, due to a newly acquired six-foot cabinet that blocks half of the doorway; a great find of Larry's, no doubt. It leaves little room for us to walk through. The small artificial Christmas tree that he erected in December still stands, further cluttering the room. It looks pathetic and small, the handful of metallic ornaments shining with the reflection from the TV. I make my way to the bedroom, passing by the Puhlers and the TV, but nothing is said between us. Sandra cranes her neck to see around me as I pass so that she doesn't miss a moment of the performance or a beat of the song, but other than that, they are oblivious to me. Or indifferent.

I throw myself onto the bed and close my eyes, imagining Marcus's smile and the way he put his arms around me and held me tight. I imagine the warmth and scent of him and his soft lips kissing me. I feel a stirring in my belly again.

I bury my head in my pillow, imagining that it's him and that we're making out and caressing each other and I can't believe how much I miss him and wish he was here.

"What are you doing?" Stephanie asks, her voice full of ridicule. I freeze and turn onto my back as though I was just lying there.

"Nothing," I say coolly. My face flames with embarrassment. She smirks and throws her sweater onto her bed.

"That's not what it looked like to me," she teases. "Missing Marcus, are you?" I throw my pillow at her and she laughs.

"Lay off," I tell her, but I mean it in a good natured way. While I'm looking at her, my eyes become fixated on the open shoebox at her feet. I realize it's my shoebox, my most treasured possession, my only tangible memories of what's been good in my life and someone has clearly gone through it! Some of its contents are spilled on the floor beside it, one photo crumpled and torn.

My face registers horror. I jump to my feet, my voice a piercing shriek. "What were you doing?!" I yell. "Who went through my stuff?"

Stephanie steps back, taken aback by my outburst.

"I was just looking," she says, shrugging.

"Just looking?!" I scream. "This is my private stuff!" I fall on my knees in front of the box, gathering the things that pepper the carpet.

"Big deal," Stephanie says.

But I pick up the lifebook Shelley made for me. Its edges are tattered from looking at it so often. The pictures of us together — biking, having picnics, at the beach, and snuggling on the couch — all start to tumble and flutter to the ground. There are concert tickets, notes that I kept from my lunch box that Shelley wrote, pictures that we drew together, even a heart-shaped locket that they bought me for my birthday. All that is precious to me is in that box and the realization that someone has gone through it without my knowledge or consent has me shaking with anger.

Then I see a ball of crinkled paper and try carefully to pull it apart. I realize it's a photo, now torn. I try to smooth the edges. It's my favourite picture. It's of Luke, Shelley, and me, and we're smiling, our arms all wrapped around each other. It was taken last summer. We had just finished riding the Ferris wheel at the amusement park, its flashing neon lights blur in the sky behind us. The picture is now so creased that our faces are mangled. There are no smiles to be seen, just a mottled mess of photo paper. I feel my insides rip with pain.

"They're dead anyway," Stephanie says, nonchalant. "It's not like they're coming back for you, ever," she finishes. I lunge at her with all of my might and we both tumble backwards into the door frame. She yelps in pain while I pummel her with my fists. I can't seem to control myself, it's as though I've come unleashed.

Stephanie's cries go unheard. In the background, Sandra's loud singing carries over the sound from the TV. I continue hitting Stephanie, pulling her hair and scratching. The TV falls silent for a split-second as the program cuts to a commercial break and Larry and Sandra finally hear the screaming and run to our room. Larry pulls me off of Stephanie, who is clutching her face and the scratches that are now bleeding. She's glaring at me like she'd like to kill me. I glare right back at her, letting her know that I'll do it again if she ever thinks of touching my stuff again. I grab the shoebox and clutch it to my body. I think of the ruined photo, of the disregard of my most precious things, and Stephanie's flippant attitude towards my belongings.

I think of the pain of losing Luke and Shelley and how robbed I feel. I think of how each day feels meaningless. I even think of the fact that Stephanie is right. They aren't coming back. Ever. But I must still hold onto everything we had. I must believe that even though they were taken from me, I was worthy of them. Because if I don't, I may never survive.

Chapter 15

The first night in my new apartment is the hardest. It has taken only minutes to unpack the few things I have and when I'm done, the place feels empty and cold. I set my shoebox on the floor next to my bed. The walls are bare except for the framed photo of everyone at Haywood, and I glance at it several times. It is taking me a while to get used to the sounds in the building. It is eerily quiet, and when there is a noise, I jump in alarm.

There's a convenience store and a grocery store just a couple of blocks away so I can pick up things I need easily. I've bought some food staples, but because of the meager budget, it isn't much. I'm grateful that I know how to cook. One of the first things I do is make myself a hot meal, which I set on my lap in the armchair in my living room. I made myself noodles and sauce and baked some fresh biscuits. I savour each bite, knowing that Shelley would be proud of me for this moment. She always wanted me to dream big and do well. And though this wouldn't have been dreaming big in her eyes, I know she'd think it was a pretty big deal that I was surviving and taking care of myself.

While I'd always enjoyed some level of privacy at Haywood, even being amongst so many others, living on my own is hard. Something about coming home to a barren, empty apartment each day reminds me of my days with my mother, Jacqueline, when I was little. I spent hours on my own back then, learning to decipher the sounds outside our small apartment. I'd try to entertain myself by singing and dancing, or by drawing pictures on any papers I could find. Now here I am, almost ten years later, resorting to the same things to keep myself company, except it doesn't feel comforting to me. It almost felt haunting, like I have come full circle with my past.

I will never be you, Jacqueline, I keep repeating to myself. *I will never be part of that life again.* It might be part promise, part aspiration, but I am determined to make more of my life and leave the ugliness of my past behind. *So many people have come in and out of my life. So few of them I have loved. So few of them have ever loved me.*

In a few short days Trina will be moving in. She is ecstatic about it. She is already packed, at least that's what she said last time we talked. Although my apartment is only a one bedroom, we'll be putting another bed beside mine and we'll share the bedroom. With Trina's meager belongings, we'll still have lots of space.

Trina also has a new job, working at a jeans retailer nearby. Although she is still in school, she only attends part-time. She kinda decided she was done with school a long time ago. How she got the job was beyond me, though I'd never tell her that. Even though Trina's appearance has softened over time, she still looks pretty rough around the edges. She hardly conjures up the image of courteous sales assistant providing superior customer service, but I know Trina and there's so much more to her than meets the eye.

Trina can't wait to get started. She's already planning which clothes she can buy on payday with her employee discount. I've tried telling her that there won't be a lot of money left over after living expenses, but she seems to think she'll be hitting the jackpot making minimum wage at an entry level job.

Work at McDonald's has been good so far. At first, it was overwhelming trying to learn all the rules of the job. On my first shift I was trained on "lobby," which was how to wash the tables and sweep the floor, change the garbage, and keep the washrooms tidy. Next I was trained on "window," which means learning how to use the front till and take orders from customers. I liked that job much better because I could actually interact with people, but I found that even though I was going as fast as I could, people were very impatient and eager to get their food and get out of there. After my first few shifts I came home tired from trying to remember everything.

I reek of oil from the deep fryers after each shift. I often wash my uniform in the sink with soap because I can't stand the smell. The nearest laundromat is blocks away and I can't afford to go down there and wash my uniform that much. I usually work the supper shift any-how, and there isn't enough time to get down there to wash clothes between the time when school ends and when I start work.

I've been getting to know some of the other employees. Most are young and starting out in their first job. Surprisingly, I'm finding that I really enjoy it. I take pride in doing my job well and my managers comment on my good work ethic. I thrive on the praise.

Although I tend to work mostly in the evenings, it sometimes varies: early mornings, afternoons, late nights. My favourite is the early morning, when the seniors come in. I am fascinated by how they come day after day, meeting their friends for coffee dates that last several hours. I make sure to remember the orders of the regulars before they can say them, and they smile in appreciation each time.

I search their faces, seeing the wisdom of their years. I hope that by that age, life will be easier. Maybe by then I will have it all figured out. I am so full of questions and have so few answers.

My least favourite shift is the late nights. I hate walking home afterwards. The restaurant has a policy where they pay for cabs for the female staff to get home after midnight, but because I live so close, I can't justify the expense. Even the two-block walk home feels harrowing at times in this neighbourhood.

While other parts of the city are quiet with residents tucked into their beds, this neighbourhood tends to come alive late at night. Homes that looked closed up and abandoned pulse with life after dark: doors and windows are left open, visitors stream in and out. People sit on the front steps or across the lawn, often drinking. There are groups of people walking around everywhere. Sounds of cars rumbling and people yelling are commonplace.

There are often domestic disputes, a lively party or bored teens up to no good. I walk quickly and determined with my hands in my pockets and my head tucked down into the hood of my jacket. I cross the street at the sign of anyone coming my way. Many nights I take a longer route to get home just to avoid groups of people.

But I've found that I've settled into a manageable kind of life. I am working hard and I have a decent place to live. I know the loneliness will be quelled in a few days when Trina arrives. Maybe things really are looking up.

Chapter 16

February 2005

I am walking with Marcus. It is late at night and the others are in the park, drinking. Marcus asked me to come with him to his house and I am thrilled to have some time alone with him without everyone watching our every move. He's gripping my hand tight and keeps kissing my temple as we walk, his tall body leaning down to me easily. I'm shivering again, both from the cold and the butterflies in my stomach. I have no idea where Marcus lives or how far it is.

We walk quite a few blocks and my feet feel frozen in my thin running shoes. It is forty below with the wind chill and my ears are searing with pain from the exposure. I'm trying to make small talk, but my lips are having a hard time forming sentences and I can feel something like ice crystals forming in my nostrils making it harder to breathe.

Marcus's long legs take huge strides, and I almost have to run to keep up with him. "We're almost there," he says to me, laughing. He must see how cold I am. He pulls me towards a rundown apartment building which has more boards than windows. The security door is broken and the light bulbs have been smashed out of the ceiling. It's dark and damp but Marcus navigates his way easily down the stairwell to his basement apartment. The carpet in the hallway is stained in so many places it's hard to figure out its original colour. I squeeze his hand a little tighter. I don't feel comfortable in this place. In fact, I feel a bit scared.

He unlocks the deadbolt and then kicks the door of his suite with his foot and motions for me to go in. It's tiny and dark. I notice right away that the walls have several holes. He flicks the light switch on and the warm glow of the small bulb casts shadows around the room. Marcus's apartment takes me by surprise. There is leather furniture lining the living room, and a big-screen TV dominating the main wall. He even has a leather dining set in the tiny dining room. There is a plush area rug in the middle of the room and a bookcase full of hundreds of CDs and DVDs against the wall. My face must register shock at the extravagant things he owns because he smirks at me and tells me to have a seat.

I sit on the couch and curl my legs under me, grateful to be out of the cold. Marcus checks his cell phone. He pulls out a bottle from the cupboard and rinses out two glasses that are sitting in the sink. I glance at the coffee table in front of me and see a box of gold jewellery, its contents spilling over the sides. I look around the room, trying to take it all in. I've never seen so many expensive things in one place before.

Marcus slides in next to me and passes me a glass. I eagerly take a sip, wanting the liquid to warm my throat and my insides. He sips his and sets it down and pulls me towards him.

"You okay?" he asks when he realizes that I'm still trembling. "Do you want to take a hot shower or something?" I shake my head and hold my glass tightly to my chest.

"Come here," he says, taking the glass from my hand and setting it on the table.

I tremble harder but Marcus holds me tighter before putting his weight on me and forcing me down until I am lying on my back on the cushions of the couch. He brings his mouth down on mine, gentle at first, his warm breath taking the chill away. I return his kiss and wrap my arms around his neck. We keep kissing, the passion building between us. He slides his hand underneath my shirt and I gasp at the feeling of his cold fingers exploring my body. My mind is racing at the thought of what we are doing and how thrilling it feels. Marcus touches me gently and I feel stirrings I've never felt before.

Marcus slides his hand down my body and I squirm at his touch. He kisses my neck and moves his mouth down to my chest at the same time. I feel scared and excited all at once, but I can't imagine telling him to stop. He kisses his way back up to my neck and then takes his arms and wraps them tightly around me, flipping us both over so that I'm beside him. He holds me close to him, his chin resting on the top of my head.

"I love you, Bernice," he says breathlessly. I melt into him, my heart thudding through my chest.

"I love you too, Marcus," I respond because he's being so sweet and gentle and he's making me feel like no one ever has. And he wants me of all people, plain, old unlovable me.

"We better go," Marcus says after what feels like a couple of hours of us cuddling. His cell phone keeps ringing and I can tell he's agitated by it every time it goes off. "Why won't anyone leave me the hell alone?" he says angrily. He helps me up from the couch, but darkness has clouded his eyes. Whoever is trying to reach him has got him in a foul mood.

"What's going on?" I ask, but Marcus just shakes me off, eager to get moving again. "I'll walk you home," he says to me.

I try to hide my disappointment at having to leave the warmth of the apartment and my alone time with Marcus. I'm not looking forward to the walk back in the cold. But Marcus holds me as we are walking and my heart skips a beat at the thought of our make-out session. How I hope it won't be our last. But he loves me … loves *ME!* So I know that it will only be the first of many.

I smile at him adoringly as we walk and he chuckles at the silly grin on my face. Every so often he stops in mid-stride and takes my head in his hands to kiss me and I feel tingly all over. We arrive at the Puhlers' much too soon.

"Goodnight, beautiful," he says, winking. I reluctantly pull away from him and tell him goodnight. He watches me enter the house before leaving. I close the door softly behind me, not wanting to wake anyone, and lean against the back of the door. I close my eyes and imagine Marcus kissing me and touching me. I imagine him telling me how much he loves me over and over again and my heart feels like it's going to burst. I think of how I've heard of people searching their whole lives for love and never finding it and how lucky I feel that at thirteen I've experienced it. For the first time, I'm in love.

Chapter 17

Trina is my very best friend. It is amazing to have her here with me. We are able to do as we please, staying up late to talk and eat ice cream sundaes. We go to the mall together and look at all of the things we'd buy if we had the money. We've started finishing each other's sentences and squabbling over the insignificant things each of us does that annoys the other. She's become the sister I've never had and I'm thrilled about it.

Even with so little free time, it's nice to have someone to share my days with. The summer is going by very quickly and I'm trying to get as many shifts in as I can before school starts. I'm getting excited at the thought of starting my classes, but nervous at how I'll do. Trina keeps telling me that I'll be fine, that I don't realize how smart I am and that I'll breeze through, but I'm not so sure.

It's Friday night. Trina and I are supposed to be having a girl's night watching a movie and eating popcorn but it's almost eleven and she isn't home yet. I've already made the popcorn and poured our drinks but the ice cubes have long since melted. I'm wearing my comfiest pajamas with my plush slippers. I'm restless staring at the clock waiting for Trina to come through the door.

Her shift ended at nine o'clock and after counting the time it takes to get to the bus stop and home, she should have been home at least an hour ago. I shove handfuls of popcorn into my mouth, but it seems tasteless when I'm so worried. I shut the lights off in the apartment and step out onto the small balcony so I can watch for her. I sit cross-legged on the floor of the balcony watching all of the activity of a Friday night. I see the constant reminder of why I hate walking home in this neighbourhood, especially after my night shifts.

I hear the brakes of the city bus in the distance and the engine of the bus as it gains momentum again. The bus stop is two blocks away, but I can hear the sound of the bus clearly on this summer night. I keep watching for Trina as far as my eye can see, but when she doesn't appear even after two buses have made their scheduled stops, I realize that something is wrong.

I slide open the patio door and step back into our apartment. I kick off my slippers and put on my shoes, not bothering to change out of my pajamas. I quickly lock the door behind me, shoving the key into my shoe. I run down the stairwell and push open the security door, breathing in the night air.

I look around the parking lot and see no one. It's quiet and very dark. Not quite sure where I'm headed or where to look, I walk down towards the bus stop, hoping to meet Trina there, though the feeling in my gut tells me it's unlikely. Several cars pass me on the street, a few of them with drunken teenagers whistling or yelling at me and my outfit. I ignore them and focus on finding Trina.

When I reach the bus stop, I feel a sense of anticipation when I see the next bus approach. A teenage boy steps off the bus, his hat pulled far down his face. Otherwise, the bus is empty. I step into the bus and ask the driver if he's seen anyone that fits Trina's description, but he shakes his head. "It's been a quiet night tonight," he tells me. "I would've remembered if she'd been on the bus."

I nod and thank him, fear flooding my system. She's always home when she says she's going to be. I turn to make my way back to the apartment, but I can't help but feel uneasy.

I decide to take another route home, near the convenience store that we like to frequent. It's two blocks in the opposite direction, but I figure that if I go that way, at least I can rule out the other place she's likely to be. Young kids are racing their bikes in the streets, even though it's so late at night. I see the glow of the convenience store sign and walk a little faster. I am only half a block away and I can see the store is buzzing with activity. Security guards pace back and forth in front of the building. At times they limit the number of customers in the store, creating a line-up of people who must wait outside for their turn until other customers have made their purchases and left.

As I'm walking, I hear a small whine and imagine it's a kitten. I slow my pace and glance down the alley that's adjacent to me, but I see nothing. I pause and hear the sound again. I look around but I can't see anything that could be making the sound. Curious, I step partway into the alley and recognize the sound. Someone is crying. It's hard to make out anything in the alley, so I follow the sound to what looks like a black garbage bag alongside a fence. Then I realize it's not a garbage bag at all but a person curled into a fetal position on the ground.

"Are you okay?" I ask, alarmed.

The cries become louder and I realize that something is very wrong. I bend over the person, but it's so hard to see anything properly in the cavernous dark of the alley.

"Are you hurt?" I ask. The person sobs and manages to say yes in a panicked voice. "I can get help," I say, thinking about the convenience store just up ahead. We could phone the police and the ambulance.

"Andy?" says a feeble voice. My blood runs cold.

"No, no, no," I say, scared. I turn the person over and search for a face. It's her. It's Trina. Although I can barely make out her features, it's definitely her. My stomach lurches with worry and anger and a million questions spill out.

"How did you get here? Who did this to you? What happened?" I ask, but Trina is groaning and sobbing and she clearly needs medical attention. I reach my hand out to touch her face and feel the wet stickiness of blood.

"I'll get help, Trina," I tell her. "Just let me run to the store," I say. "I'll be right back, I promise." But she cries and grabs onto me, not wanting me to leave her. I start to cry and tell her everything will be alright, but that I need to get help. I wrestle my body away from her grip and run as fast as ever to the line-up that has formed at the convenience store.

"Excuse me, but I need you to call the police for me, and an ambulance," I tell the security guard. He looks me up and down, amused by the sight of me in my pajamas and raises an eyebrow in suspicion.

"My friend ... she's been seriously hurt and she needs an ambulance," I shout. My voice sounds high and ragged. He scratches his neck and looks into the store as though he hasn't heard a word I've said.

"You're not just trying to get into the store now, are you?" he says seriously. He looks back at the line-up of customers standing outside the store. I stare at him in amazement.

"Look, please, my friend is hurt! Could you please call for help? She's just around the corner here," I scream, pointing in the direction of the alley. When he doesn't lift his radio, I turn to the others, desperate now. "Please! Does anyone have a phone? We need an ambulance and police here right away," I beg. I feel like I could hit this man who seems so unmoved by what I'm saying. I wave my blood-covered hand in the air so they can see it.

A woman finally registers the panic in my voice and pulls out a cell phone from her purse.

"Here, I can call for you," she says. She starts to dial, but her fingers fumble over the keys. I shuffle impatiently until the call goes through. The customers in the line-up listen, curious. I thank the woman and then run back towards the alley. Already I can hear sirens approaching from somewhere. I run as fast as I can until my breathing is heavy and uneven.

Trina is in the same position that I left her in, still whimpering with pain.

"It's okay," I tell her. "Help is on the way." The sirens become louder and louder until finally I see the circling red flash of the ambulance casting eerie glows onto the back fences in the alley. I watch as the paramedics tend to her and get her strapped onto the stretcher. In the light from the inside of the ambulance I gasp when I finally see her face. She is bruised and bloody, her left eyelid so swollen that I can't even see her eye. She is even missing teeth. She is moaning and drifting in and out of consciousness and I try to soothe her. Two police officers ask me one question after another, but I don't have the answers to any of them. I don't know who did this to her, how or why it happened. I only know that my best friend is broken and bleeding and I can't make sense of it.

One of the paramedics invites me to ride with them to the hospital. The police agree to meet us at the hospital so that they can question Trina. I climb into the ambulance and sit holding Trina's hand, but I'm not sure she even knows I am there. She has an oxygen mask on her face, machines monitoring her vital signs. I shiver at the sight of her, wondering how this could have happened. I think of all of the times I walked home at night and how I'd always made it home safely. I'd been fearful at times, but nothing had ever happened. And now Trina is lying here, severely injured. Somehow I can't help but feel like it should be me lying here instead of her.

The ride to the hospital seems to take forever, but once we reach the emergency room everything moves quickly. Trina is whisked away and I'm left holding her bloody sweater. A nurse takes me to get her admitted and the police officers from the scene wait for me to finish. I'm terrified not knowing how Trina is doing, hoping she'll be okay.

I sit on one of the hard plastic chairs in the waiting room. The people around me have drawn-out looks on their faces, either tolerating their pain while they wait to see a doctor or eager for news about their loved ones. I swallow several times, trying to keep tears from coming. Who could have done this to her?

An hour later, a nurse calls for me from the hallway.

"Are you Andy?" she asks when I stand.

"Yes," I say breathlessly. My heart is pounding; my hands are slick with sweat.

"You can go in and see her now," the nurse says. "She's asking for you." I nod numbly and follow her down the corridor.

"She'll need a lot of rest, but she'll be okay," the nurse says. I pull back the curtain that surrounds the bed and slip in quietly. Trina has her eyes closed, half of her face swollen beyond recognition. She is still hooked up to oxygen. Dried blood mats her hair and dots her skin. Despite the horrific appearance of her face, she looks peaceful as she's resting. The nurse enters and writes a couple of things on a clipboard.

"We've given her something for the pain, so she'll be more comfortable," she tells me. I nod again, unable to say a word, stunned by Trina's appearance. I pull a chair closer to her bedside and feel for her hand. I stare at her features, tears falling faster than I can brush them away. Trina stirs and I feel a slight squeeze from her hand.

"I'm here, Trina," I say softly.

One of the police officers from the scene enters and asks me again what I know. They've been able to discern that it was a group of teens, perhaps gang members, who beat Trina. I bristle at the officer's questions, which keep leading back to whether or not Trina has been involved in any gang activity or if she has any connections to people who might be involved in the attack. I explain that we've been living together and working since leaving Haywood House, that I'm her best friend, and that she isn't involved in any funny business, but the officer seems skeptical. I guess it's easy to assume that since we've never had a stable home life, girls like us must be trouble. I answer the questions the best that I can, but it's only Trina who really knows what happened.

Trina is still dozing when the officer leaves. I caress her hand and lay my head on the bed near her body. I'm suddenly exhausted. I glance at the clock above the bed and see that it is four in the morning. I want to fight sleep so that I can attend to Trina, but in the end my eyelids become so heavy that I give in. She's going to need me tomorrow.

Chapter 18

April 2005

Marcus has been acting strange for weeks now. He is either crazy about me and showering me with love or he disappears for days on end, sometimes ignoring me when I see him out on the street. I feel confused and hurt until he kisses me and tells me how much he loves me, how beautiful I am, and then I know things are okay.

The days feel so long without Marcus and I sit day-dreaming during class, imagining the two of us together. It has been six days since I've seen him last, and I'm uneasy about the whole thing. *Maybe I should find him and go and talk to him. Find out what's really going on,* I think to myself. When the bell rings for afternoon recess, I take my jacket from the hook and close the door to my locker, deciding that I am going to track him down.

Stephanie shoots me a dirty look from across the hall, her eyes following my every move. She watches me head for the doors, and I just know that she's going to rat me out for leaving school before anyone has a chance to real-ize I'm not there. It's not like she hasn't done it a million times too, but we are barely talking these days; she still thinks I overreacted about her going through my things.

The truth is I don't want her near my things because I don't trust her one bit, but that's kind of hard to do when you share a room with each other. Hunter has been telling me to end it with Marcus. He's never been happy about us seeing each other. I don't get what all the fuss is. I've asked him if he is jealous, but he just shrugs me off saying that Marcus isn't the kind of guy I should be with.

What does Hunter know? He sure sucks up to Marcus and bows down to him when he sees him. Marcus is used to getting respect from the other kids on the street, and that's something I admire about him. I feel proud to be his girlfriend, even when he shuts down and ignores me. I know life is tough; Marcus must be going through some things.

I head to the Puhlers' so I can grab something to eat and freshen up. I have a long, hot shower and take extra care to do my hair and makeup so that I look my best when I find Marcus. It takes me a couple of hours to get ready. I dab perfume on my wrists, behind my ears, and between my breasts, hoping I'm irresistible to him. *I just know we can work things out. I can help him with whatever is bothering him,* I think.

I walk to Marcus's apartment, careful to sidestep the spray of shattered glass that litters the entrance to the building. Half of the glass in the security door has been smashed out, which seems odd to me since the lock on the door doesn't work anyway. I head for the stairs to the basement, my steps crunching over shards of glass. I knock on the apartment door several times, but there's no answer. Further down the hall, the door to another suite opens and an elderly Asian man sticks his head out.

"Go away," he says in broken English. "No safe for you," he tells me, waving his hand. I step back in alarm. What could have happened here? And where is Marcus?

I step back over the glass to go outside and decide to head to the tracks. Chances are some of the kids are gathered there and I'll find out where he is. I shove my hands in my pockets and head for the park. I start planning how I can make him feel better when I see him. Night descends quickly at this time of year and although there isn't much snow, the temperature drops quickly in the evenings.

As I enter the park I see most of the regular crowd sitting and drinking. Many of the kids are high and greet me enthusiastically.

"Just in time," Hunter says. He holds out an unopened twenty-sixer of whiskey. I smile and take it, grateful for the company.

"Have you seen Marcus?" I ask, but Hunter shrugs, indifferent. I turn and ask the others, but everyone shrugs. I watch another couple snuggle and kiss on a patch of grass and it makes me ache for Marcus. If I could just find him, I'd be able to cheer him up. Why does he pull away when I love him so much? I scan the park for him but see nothing. I chug the bottle of whiskey and lay on my back on the grass. The sky starts blurring; the sounds around me fade.

It gets harder to keep my eyes open so I close them for a few moments. I listen to the chatter and laughter of everyone around me until I hear yelling in the distance. I open my eyes and look around. A girl about my age is dressed in a short dress and heels, her hair piled high on her head. Her eyes are cast downward as she hugs herself protectively. The girl starts to cry and the next thing I see is a male figure punch her in the face. She clutches her mouth and doubles over in pain, but the person kicks her and she falls to the ground. He pulls the purse off her shoulder and rummages through it, spilling its contents. All I can see is him pocketing bills while the other items roll carelessly away. He drops the purse on the ground and spits on the girl before walking away. We all watch as she lies on the grass, weeping.

I look to everyone who is standing around watching, wondering why no one is doing anything to stop him or help this girl. Instead, a bunch of the boys laugh and turn to follow the figure who is heading back towards the street. Stephanie is even smiling and shaking her head in disbelief. I'm confused at what's going on. What did this girl do? Why did this guy treat her that way?

"She's always trying to get out of turning tricks." Stephanie says it like it's no big deal, but she sees the confusion on my face. She raises her eyebrows in surprise and says, "She's Marcus's newest girl and she doesn't like hooking." Hunter nudges Stephanie to be quiet.

"What?!" she says to him. "How else does she think we get our cash around here?" Hunter coughs and gives Stephanie a small push.

"That wasn't Marcus," I say, defiant.

"It sure as hell was," Stephanie says, pointing in his direction. I look past her and see the tall figure in the distance. Although I want to believe that it wasn't Marcus, I know she's right.

"Marcus takes good care of us," Stephanie says, smiling, clearly satisfied with having told me. Is that what

Marcus is really about? He's a pimp? And Stephanie is hooking too? I don't want to come across so naive but Stephanie can see right through me.

"Oh, Marcus likes you, honey," she says, winking at me. I feel sick all at once, a combination of the alcohol and what I've just learned. "You didn't think he actually loved you and wanted you for himself, did you?" she smirks.

But the world is spinning around me, her words tumbling in my head. I look at the crying girl trying to scoop up the contents of her purse and shiver.

"You're next, Bernice," Stephanie sings, her laughter echoing through the park like an evil cackle.

But it can't be, I tell myself. That may be true for the other girls, but Marcus loves me. I decide to head in the same direction as Marcus. I need to talk to him and reassure myself that what we have is real, that Marcus feels differently about me. I run across the park, calling for Marcus. It looks as though he's headed home and he doesn't turn to acknowledge me. I continue to follow him, sure that he'll turn and wait for me but he doesn't. I watch as he goes into the building. I break into a run, eager to talk to him. I step back over the broken glass and run down the stairs to his door. I knock, hoping that he'll answer but he doesn't come. "Marcus, I know you're in there," I say. "Will you please let me in?"

After a couple of minutes, Marcus opens the door. His jaw is set, his eyes dark. "What?" he says impatiently.

"Are you okay?" I ask, though I know that clearly he is not. He steps aside so that I can enter and shuts the door behind us.

"What happened?" I ask. But Marcus is almost shaking with anger and doesn't want to talk. He sits on the couch, his head bent over his knees. He's rubbing his face and his hair. I sit next to him and start rubbing his back. He tenses up even more. I stroke his hair, and kiss his back. Marcus turns to me and pulls me towards him. He kisses me hard on the mouth, his lips crushing mine. I let out a small yelp but it seems to please him. He kisses me without stopping until my lips feel sore and bruised. I try to push Marcus away, but he pins himself down on me until I am unable to move.

Marcus starts pulling down my pants. I squirm to avoid his grasp, but he continues. "Marcus," I say, but it comes out garbled because he is kissing me so hard. Marcus puts his weight on me, until I can hardly breathe and I realize that he's fumbling with his belt buckle. My mind is racing, my heart pounding. Why can't Marcus and I just talk about things? Why won't he slow down?

I try to tell myself that this will make Marcus feel better, that he'll be happy and relaxed and ready to talk when it's over and that everything will be okay, but Marcus is hurting me. I try pushing him off again, but he has me pinned. My lips hurt from the force of his kisses.

"No, Marcus, no," I manage in between Marcus's kisses, but he ignores me. "Marcus," I say again, squirming beneath him.

"Stay still," he orders me.

"No!" I tell him again, my eyes pleading. "Please stop, Marcus! I love you but I'm not ready for this," I say. Marcus sits up over me, allowing me to finally breathe properly. I look up at him, relieved that he has stopped. I look into his eyes, but they are cold. He looks me up and down and starts unzipping his pants. Realizing what he's doing I shake my head.

"No, please, Marcus!" But before I know it his fist connects with the side of my face, leaving me almost delirious. The throbbing pain clouds my mind, the room becomes fuzzy. I start whimpering, knowing that Marcus is not going to stop. Marcus rips down my underwear and positions himself. My body trembles with fear.

The next thing I know I feel a plunge of pain that feels like my insides are being torn up. I cry out in pain, hot tears streaming down the sides of my temples. Marcus thrusts himself back and forth, each movement sending searing pains through my body. The room spins and turns to black at times, and my heart shatters into a million pieces.

Finally Marcus rolls off me, says nothing, and walks away. He grabs his coat and heads for the door. My pants are around my ankles, one leg of my underwear torn completely. I hear the door slam and I know that Marcus has left. I reach down for my pants, scared to move. I start sobbing, my body shaking uncontrollably. I try to sit up, but the pain is hot and unbearable. Warm blood stains the insides of my thighs and sticky streaks of blood mark the cushion of the leather couch.

I pull my pants up, my legs wobbly and unsure. My lips and face feel bruised. I take small steps to the doorway, my vision blurred from my tears. I shut the door behind me and climb the stairs slowly, clutching my stomach because I feel like I'm going to vomit.

I hear the crunch of the shattered glass under my feet again; I replay the words of the Chinese man warning me of my safety just hours before and picture Marcus sitting over me. The combination of these visions swirl in my head and the agony of what has happened to me becomes almost too much to bear. Unable to push open the security door, I step back and sit on the step, pain vibrating up my back when I sit down. I hold my head in my hands, sobbing. How could I be so sure of someone's love and be so wrong? How could I think that anyone would love me?

I imagine that I am dead, floating weightlessly in the air of some strange world, feeling nothing. I glance down at the pieces of broken glass and pick out a long, thin shard with a pointy end. I look at it like it's my saviour. I run the edge of the glass across my forearms until I see a thin stream of blood. I decide I like it. The sight pleases me, gives me new pain to focus on and makes me numb again. I run the shard up and down my arms, making my body as broken as my spirit. I imagine myself dead, lying in a pool of blood in this dark, damp stairwell and cry even harder.

Chapter 19

It's been weeks since Trina's attack. Although she has no idea who attacked her and why, she hasn't been the same since. She is home with me, but she hasn't been back to work since the attack. She will barely get out of bed and when she does, it's to light a cigarette and sit on the balcony, staring into space.

I've tried talking to her, tried finding out how I can help, but Trina has completely shut down. I wish she'd just open up to me, after all, I am her best friend. I'm also worried about the fact that she hasn't been working. Even though many of our expenses are paid for and Trina hasn't exactly been eating much for weeks now, I still can't help but worry.

Her boss has been calling, wondering if and when Trina's coming to work. Her boss had given her six weeks off to recover and take care of herself, but it is now eight weeks and Trina has yet to touch base with her again. I'm afraid if she doesn't talk to her boss soon, there won't be a job for her to go back to.

But working is the least of her problems. It's like Trina has disappeared and left a shell of a girl behind.

Seeing her lost in herself makes me nervous. There are no late night talks, no giggles, and no making meals together, nothing but silence.

I think back to what I felt like after Marcus raped me. I shut down, too, and wouldn't talk to anyone. No matter how much I try to tell Trina that I know how she is feeling, she still won't let me into her thoughts and feelings. And that is the worst part, because I remember the pain I felt back then, how dead I felt inside. Knowing that Trina won't let me in, when she needs someone to be there for her the most, really sucks.

I started my first term of university. I love that I can get lost in a crowd, that no one really knows who I am. There are too many of us shuffling in and out of class each day. I'm taking four classes: English, Biology, Sociology, and Psychology. The classes are held in large lecture theatres, sometimes with hundreds of students. It's overwhelming and I'm trying to do my best. It's stressful trying to keep up with school and work. Between reading my textbooks, writing papers, and juggling long shifts at work, I feel like I'm gone all the time.

Today I'm rushing to get home and be at work on time, much like every other day of the school week. I race up the stairs to our apartment, fully expecting to see Trina curled up on her mattress in our room or sitting on the chair on the balcony. When I walk through the apartment and don't see her anywhere, I breathe a sigh of relief. *She must be back at work*, I think to myself. *It's about time*. I quickly slip on my uniform and gather my name tag and visor.

I race across the parking lot of our building and jog to work. It is 4:53 and I start in seven minutes. Not ever having been late before, I don't want this to be the first time. I'm jumping over parking medians and running down the streets, hoping to get to the restaurant in time. I round the last corner at the edge of the restaurant's parking lot and sigh with relief knowing that I'll be in the building in mere seconds. I take a quick glance to my left and continue through the parking lot.

The alarming screech of brakes and a flash of metal fill the space around me. I stop, stunned. A young man driving a small car has just slammed on the brakes, narrowly missing me by inches. I put my arm out and my fingers touch the hood of the car. My heart is pounding uncontrollably, my breath ragged and quick. The driver steps out of the car, visibly shaken, and rushes to my side.

"Oh my God," he says in between gulps of air. "Are you alright?!" I nod numbly. "I almost hit you! It's like you came out of nowhere," he says.

I realize that it's mostly my fault. I'm in a hurry, running through the parking lot, the glare of the sun obstructing my vision when there's a car hurtling towards me. I put my hands on the hood of the car to steady myself, anxious to get my bearings and get into work.

"I, I, have to go …" I stammer. But I'm a bit woozy and the driver can see that. He places his warm, shaking hand on my shoulder, his eyes filled with concern. Suddenly my manager comes running out to see if I'm okay.

"Andy! We saw everything!" he says, incredulous. Before I know it, there are multiple people surrounding me to make sure I'm alright. I hear people admonishing the driver for almost hitting me and not watching where he was going.

"No," I say. "It was all my fault. I just ran out in front of him. I didn't see the car and I just ran out," I repeat. When everyone is confident that I'm truly alright, my manager puts his arm around me to guide me inside the restaurant. I turn to take another look at the driver, who is still staring at me with concern. He looks to be about my age, maybe a bit older. His sandy coloured hair is gleaming in the sunlight. I give him a smile and a wave, hoping to reassure him and he gives me a wide, relieved smile in return before getting back into his car.

"Thank goodness you're okay," my manager says, shaking his head. I nod, thinking how it could have been much worse.

The rest of my shift is relatively uneventful and after four hours, I punch out my time card and take off my visor. Being that it is fall, it's dark outside already. I rub my arms in the chilly night air, a bit uneasy about my walk home. Since Trina's attack, I'm even more on edge when I'm walking alone. I wave to my coworkers through the drive-thru window and walk across the parking lot. Just as I'm about to step onto the sidewalk, I hear a voice.

"Can I give you a lift home?" someone asks. I turn to see who it is. It's the guy who almost hit me earlier. He looks nervous and uncomfortable. "Please, it's the least I can do," he says. "I'll get you there safely, I promise," he says. I stop and study his face. He has kind eyes, bright pools of blue that are looking at me as though he'd give me the world if he could just to make things right. He is clean-cut and handsome, long and lean, and staring at me intently. I don't know who is sizing up the other more, me or him.

He's standing by his little blue car, motioning for me to get in. "How did you know when I was off?" I ask pointedly. He shuffles and grins at me, sheepish.

"I didn't. I decided to come back here about an hour ago hoping to talk to you to apologize again. I asked another worker when you were off and she figured it was at eight. I thought I'd wait so that I could try and make things up to you," he finishes.

"Look, it's not like you hit me," I say to him. "So you came close … that doesn't mean you need to stalk me now to make amends. This is a little creepy," I say, though I can tell by the look on his face that this wasn't his intention and he's clearly embarrassed.

I realize the absurdity of getting into this stranger's car, of all the things that could happen to me, but I see the look on his face and feel strangely safe. I look around the lot and decide to get in. It's colder out than I expected, and the thought of walking isn't very appealing to me tonight. "I'm Austin," he says holding out his hand, his face registering relief. I give his hand a shake and smile.

"Andy," I say.

"I'm so sorry for what happened earlier," he tells me. "I haven't been able to forget it. I promise you, I'm no creep. I just felt like it would be a gentlemanly thing to do," he says. I laugh, thinking that I've never met a true gentleman, until possibly this very day. He waits for me to buckle my seatbelt and then slowly backs out of the parking space. I can see the manager of the restaurant staring out of the drive-thru window at us, obviously shocked to see me in the car that almost hit me just hours earlier.

"I can imagine I'm going to hear about this tomorrow," I say, chuckling as we see the manager's gaping mouth. Austin gives me a nervous smile.

"I hope this doesn't get you into any trouble," he says. I shake my head, knowing that it'll be fine.

"I'm only a couple of blocks away," I say to Austin. He's driving very carefully, focused on the road. I give him my address and look at his face. His eyes are fixated on the road, his hands gripping the wheel. "Do you work or go to school?" I ask him, hoping for some small talk. After all, if this guy really is a gentleman instead of a creep, then talking with him would be nice.

"Both," he says. "I'm in my fourth year at the University of Saskatchewan. Drama major."

I nod, impressed.

"I also work at the public library part-time," he tells me.

"I love the library," I answer, and he glances at me in surprise.

"That's not something I usually hear," he smiles.

"It's true," I say. "I've always loved books. They're like an escape to another world."

He nods in agreement.

"I'm at the U of S too. Only my first year though." I pause. "I don't know what I'm going to major in exactly," I admit.

Austin seems pleased that I'm in school too, that we share a couple of things in common. His car pulls up to my apartment building and I can't help but feel disappointed. "Andy, again, I'm so sorry for what happened earlier ..." he stammers.

"I'm fine," I reassure him. "Besides, you've already made it up to me. Thanks for giving me a ride home!" I open the car door, reluctant to get out. Talking to Austin has been nice.

"Maybe I'll see you around?" he asks. I smile and nod, hoping that he's right.

I shut the car door and wave before walking to the apartment entrance. Austin waits to make sure I'm inside before waving and pulling away. It's crazy to think this of a complete stranger, but my heart does a little skip at the thought of him. Maybe he's a gentleman after all.

Chapter 20

May 2005

The house is quiet this morning. Everyone is still sleeping. I'm lying in bed staring at the mattress slats of the top bunk. I imagine tying a rope or a long piece of fabric to the slats and securing it around my neck. In mere minutes I'd be dead.

It's my fourteenth birthday today. But today won't be a day of celebration. I can't seem to breathe, I'm so sad. I feel like there is little to live for, that I really have no future ahead of me. I imagine how little fanfare there would be if I died, how so few would notice my absence. Perhaps no one would come to my funeral. A life wouldn't seem well lived if there weren't any attendees at the funeral, now would it?

I turn over to face the wall, examining the chips in the paint and the gouges in the wall. It's dirty and there are still tiny patches of old wallpaper remaining. It's like someone decided that it was too much work to remove it all, so they just painted the wall anyway.

Out of the corner of my eye I see something silver and shiny beside my pillow. I grasp it with my closest hand. It's a safety pin. I roll it around in my fingers, feeling the cold metal. I open the clasp and prick my finger on the edge. It's a quick, sharp poke. I poke my other finger, smiling at the sensation. I run the edge of the needle end up and down the length of my thumb, feeling a tingle from the needle's point. I don't know what it is about it, but I'm fixated by this sensation in my body.

I continue down the length of my arm to where the skin is softest. I run the edge closer and deeper until a scratch forms. It stings a bit, but I like the feeling. I press harder, watching as the edge slices through the skin until blood appears. There is something triumphant about seeing the blood, as though I've accomplished something. The initial pain is replaced with numbness. I feel powerful and in control. I can make my body feel physical pain and then make it go numb again. I switch hands and run the safety pin down my other arm, creating a matching line. I suck in my breath as I press it into my skin, but each cut feels like a release.

I hear Stephanie stir in her sleep and I quickly hide the safety pin inside my fist. I pull down my pajama sleeves and cover the evidence. When the room is quiet again, I slip the safety pin underneath my mattress for safekeeping. I examine the red scratches, which are now throbbing. I run my finger over them but the pain is subsiding. I take another deep breath and feel incredibly calm and centred.

I've decided I'm going to leave this place today. I've packed my bag and hidden it underneath my bed. I can't bear to be here anymore. There is no one to talk to about what I'm going through or how I'm feeling. Seeing

Hunter and Stephanie just reminds me of everything that's happened and what life will really be like if I stay.

Everyone is still meeting in the park or out by the train tracks. I haven't been there in weeks. I can't bear the thought of running into Marcus. Since Stephanie and I still aren't talking, Hunter has been keeping his distance too. I'm sure it's out of allegiance to Stephanie. He'll glance my way often when he's around though, so I'm sure he's figured out that something's up.

I don't have a plan yet. I figure I'll walk out of here and make my way across the city to a safer park where no one knows me. Or perhaps I'll go down to the riverbank and find myself a cozy nook among the trees. I know there are no other places for me to go. When my caseworker discovers that I'm gone, I'll have to lay pretty low. They'll be interviewing the Puhlers and Stephanie and Hunter, trying to determine where I might have gone. There'll be a missing persons report filed and a search will be held.

This is where I'll have to be my craftiest; I don't want anyone to find me again. I've got nowhere to go, no one to trust. I'll have to find a way to make it on my own. I've taken a towel and a small fleece blanket from the Puhlers and squished them into my backpack. They'll have to do for now. Luckily it's getting warmer outside and I'll have a few months to plan out what I'll do when fall approaches and the weather cools.

I have thirty-three dollars to my name and my ratty looking shoebox, which is more precious to me than any amount of money. I've also been stashing granola bars when I get the chance and I've got a decent pile stocked up. I haven't been eating much for days though, so I'm not too worried about how I'll feed myself.

I lift the mattress and retrieve my safety pin. I slide it into my pants pocket, grateful that I have it. I've been using anything with a sharp edge to cut myself. I've used glass, steak knives, and razors, the tabs on soda cans, nails, and even utility blades I've found on construction sites. I've got marks up and down my arms, the flabby part of my belly, and the fleshy insides of my thighs; anywhere where I can grab some skin and experiment. The cuts are different colours and shapes, in various states of healing. Fresh cuts thrill me; I envision my pain oozing through the cuts with my blood. Each slice feels like a release, like I'm emptying the ugly parts of myself.

Chapter 21

Lucky for me, Austin has been coming in to the restaurant every night for coffee after the library closes. He tells me he needs the caffeine to help him stay awake to study, but I know he's coming in to see me. We even met on campus once. He's very dedicated to school, which impresses me. I haven't met a young man so interested in furthering his education, and in his future. Most of the boys I grew up with barely got through their classes. It would be a surprise if they showed up regularly.

Austin is actually from the west coast. He's been in Saskatoon for eight years now. He moved here just before he started high school. Although he'd had a good childhood, his dad ended up leaving him and his mom when he was in junior high. After that, he grew even closer to his mom and became very protective of her. When his dad never called again, he grew used to the fact that it was just going to be him and his mom. Then just a year later, she got cancer and the disease spread so quickly, there was little anyone could do.

When she passed away, Austin was sent to live with his grandma in Saskatoon. His grandma was a lot like his mother and they formed a close bond quickly, both grieving for the woman they had lost. The day after his high school graduation, Austin's grandma passed away of a massive heart attack. The grief almost did him in, but he hung in there and decided that his mom and grandma would have wanted him to work hard and continue on.

His grandma's estate was left to him, so this afforded him the chance to go to school debt-free and live in her home. He takes his classes very seriously because he knows that his opportunity was born from great loss. Austin is determined to make his mom and grandma proud. He has applied for a Masters program at the University of Regina and is hoping to be starting school there this fall.

Despite our different childhoods, we actually have quite a bit in common. We both grieve for the people who loved us most. Our dads aren't in the picture, and in my case, my mom isn't either. Listening to Austin talk about when he was younger and had his dad makes me sad. I think he's got it tougher than me because his dad cared at some point. He wasn't always an absent father. Knowing that your dad once cared about you and spent time with you and then left, never to call again … that's got to be harder. At least mine never cared from day one.

Austin and I have even had our first kiss. A soft, gentle, and loving kiss that will go down in history as my best kiss ever. I know this because I've never experienced anything like it. Austin is protective of me too, but in a good way. He has said he likens me to a broken little bird that just needs to find my wings again. I like that.

He's very intelligent. We have deep conversations about current events, philosophical issues, making sense of our pasts. I tell him all about Haywood House, the staff and the girls, how they're like family to me. Most of the people I know that have had a painful past just try to bury it and do something to numb the pain. Trying to come to terms with it is so much harder, but so much more freeing. I've never been able to talk to someone like this. I feel challenged and excited by our talks. It's been a long time since I've felt loved. We have a pure and innocent, satisfying love. The real deal.

Trina hasn't been around much. I try to talk to her whenever she's around, but she's barely responsive. It's true that I've been spending most of my free time with Austin and I'm not home a lot, but even then, I'm not sure it would make much of a difference. In my frustration of watching Trina's life spiral downward, I've almost given up on her. She's back to her sullen moods, just like when she first came to Haywood. I've tried talking and reaching out to her, but it doesn't seem to help. At times it feels easier to leave her alone and give her space.

There's a special program at the library that Austin has encouraged me to attend. It's an opportunity for young writers to showcase their work. I was terrified to join, but the leader of the group has been so supportive. She makes me feel like writing out my thoughts and feelings and telling my story releases so much of my pain. There is supposed to be a performance night at one of the big bookstores in the city. Each of the participants will read from some of their work. I've decided to face my fears and participate. Austin is thrilled for me and excited for the performance.

For the first time, I really feel like my life is coming together. I've got people who love me and want the best for me, and for once, I really want the best for myself. I want to do well. I want people around me. I've created my own definition of family, one that doesn't include blood relatives. And that's okay.

Austin picks me up from work and kisses me on the cheek when I get into my seat. "How was your day?" he asks. I'm tired and sweaty and anxious to get home to relax for the evening.

"Better now," I tell him. Seeing him after a long day is like a warm blanket around me. Warm, comforting, protective.

"Want to watch a movie or something tonight?" he asks. I nod in agreement and we decide to head to the convenience store to get some snacks.

I'm so tired that I start feeling cranky and out of sorts. I don't mean to take it out on Austin, but he's the only one with me and I'm having a hard time holding it inside. If there's one thing I learned from counselling, holding in your emotions is toxic behaviour and everything has to come out at sometime in some way. In the past, cutting myself became my ultimate release, a way to let out all of my pain. But I'm healthier now, so I have to allow my emotions to come out and make peace with them. Today, I don't know what's wrong exactly, but I'm just not feeling like myself.

At the store, Austin senses my mood and tries to comfort me by putting his arm around me. I shrink from him a bit and see hurt flash in his eyes. "It'll be okay," he whispers, though he doesn't quite know what's wrong or whether he might be to blame.

We stand in line to pay for our snacks. I'm tapping my foot impatiently, restless and uneasy. I don't know what has got me so bugged right now. It's a Friday night and the store is busy and I can hardly stand in line. There are groups of teens talking in the parking lot, and people loitering around the store. It's a bustling place and all I can think of is how badly I want to get out of there.

"Can I meet you in the car?" I ask Austin.

He smoothes my hair with his hand and smiles. "Of course." He hands me his car keys and I can feel him watching me as I make my way to the doorway. I just want to get home and into my pajamas so that I can snuggle with Austin and tune out the rest of the world.

I swing open the door and step out onto the pavement. It's hot and humid and the air feels heavy, almost sucking the air from my lungs. The car is parked in the last spot at the edge of the store. Sitting on the sidewalk with her back against the building is a woman, dirty and disheveled. Her clothing is ripped and worn, her thin body trembling. Her knees are up to her chest and her head rests on her knees. She's rocking gently back and forth. I can smell her from a couple of feet away.

This area is full of panhandlers and transient people. I glance at her with concern, knowing full well what it was like to live on the streets, enduring the elements and trying to get by without money or food. I watch as people stare at her with disdain, stepping past her as though her situation is contagious. I reach into my purse for my wallet, knowing that I don't have much money myself but that this person needs it more than I do. Austin is just coming out of the store and he looks at me with curiosity as I head towards her.

"Here, take this," I say to her. I'm holding out a ten dollar bill. Much more money than anyone has ever given me at one time. The woman continues rocking back and forth, her matted and oily hair the only part of her head I can see.

"Ma'am?" I say, hoping I can get her attention. She lifts her head up and her glazed eyes try to focus on me. My breath gets caught in my throat; an audible gasp escapes my lips. I put my hand on the side of the building to steady myself, my heart thudding wildly in my chest.

Flashbacks and memories collide, fighting for space in my head. It's been over a decade since I've seen her, but this dirty, smelly, drug addicted and most likely homeless woman is definitely her. I'd recognize her face anywhere, its profile haunting both my dreams and my nightmares. She reaches for my outstretched hand, but instead of grasping the bill, she grabs my fingers. I feel like I'm in a trance, not sure if I'm conscious or if this moment is real. I search her eyes for a hint of recognition, but in a brief second, she lets go of my fingers to fumble for the bill.

I realize that she has no idea who I am. "Take this," I say gently. I place the bill into her probing fingers and press into her palm. "You need it more than I do," I say. She jerks her hand back quickly, as though scared that I might change my mind and try to grab it back. She smiles wide at me and I see that she is now missing a couple of teeth. I stare at her for a moment longer before stepping off the sidewalk. Austin is standing at the driver's side door, watching me, a puzzled look on his face.

"Let's go," I say. I get into the car, fasten my seatbelt, and stare straight ahead.

"What's going on?" Austin asks. He looks at the woman who is rocking back and forth again, her head resting back onto her knees, and then back at me. He starts wiping the tears that are cascading down my cheeks. "Andy?" he says. I look up at the woman, unsure of how to make sense of this moment.

"That woman," I tell him. "She's my mother."

· ·

Chapter 22

June 2005

It's been three weeks since I ran away from the Puhlers'. Though I am sure the police are looking for me, I've found it harder to remain undiscovered by Marcus and the rest of the group. It's hard to find a place to hide out when all the ones I really know used to be our regular hideaways.

I've been sleeping in a deep line of shrubs just beyond Gabriel Dumont Park, in a fairly dense part of the riverbank. Luckily the riverbank stretches for several kilometres and there are areas that are pretty remote from the city. I've dug out some of the soil with my hands to make a little trench to lay my body in. The shrubs are large and thick with leaves, so I'm fairly protected from the elements. The nights are still pretty cold. My body throbs with a piercing ache that doesn't seem to subside even with my constant shivering.

I've been walking up the trail to the nearest residential neighbourhood. It is home to some of the oldest houses in the city, vast character homes that ooze charm and sophistication. The only people I see early in the morning are the gardeners and the landscapers who are working in the yards and they don't pay me much attention.

I walk several blocks to the nearest shopping area. I take turns using the bathroom at the corner cafe, the gas station, and the medical building each day, hoping that I don't become too familiar to anyone. I scrub my face and arms and do a quick wipe of my privates, hoping that I stay clean enough not to draw attention. I even do a quick wash of my hair in the sink with the soap in the dispenser, reminding me of when I was little and would do it at school because I so rarely bathed at home.

I haven't come very far, have I? I say to myself. Here I am, years later, still washing my hair in a public restroom with liquid soap and a poor rinse, hoping that I can dry it and come out looking clean and put together before anyone walks in on me.

Maybe this is all I was ever meant to be, I tell myself. I stare at the dried blood all over my arms, scabs of varying sizes mottling my arms. I think of every cut I've made, how each memory is etched into a part of my flesh, like a roadmap of my life and my pain.

My stomach throbs with hunger and I realize how thin and sickly I look. I'm running free though, and living on my own terms feels better than being at the Puhlers'. I think of Stephanie and Hunter and the rest of the kids. They're probably all looking out for me. I'm always looking over my shoulder, hoping no one spots me. I can feel how anxious I'm becoming, like time is running out.

The nights are the worst. The people who wander the riverbank at night aren't always the most desirable and I find myself frozen in fear when I hear others rummaging nearby. There are often groups of teens drinking and throwing bottles at trees. I don't try to befriend anyone. I don't want anyone knowing I'm here. At times, I can hear the voices of people I sense are up to no good and I lay trembling, hoping that I'll remain safe in my little trench.

At night the mosquitoes have their way with me, leaving flaring bumps up and down my skin. The bites are hard to scratch because of all of my cuts. One swipe with my nails and I'm bleeding all over again. I don't like the blood that oozes from my scabs. It turns my stomach and makes me feel ill. It doesn't give me the thrill of a fresh cut, when the blood trickles freely with the pain.

I ran out of food days ago. Luckily with it being practically summer now, people are eating at the picnic tables and they rarely pick up all of their garbage before they leave. Families with young children are my favourite. The kids drop morsels of food everywhere when they eat. I sit quietly, flipping through one of my books, pretending to be engrossed in reading and watching the river. Once they leave, I quickly walk over to the site and gather whatever I can find. Sometimes there are full portions of food left on the tables. Often I gather handfuls of Cheezies or cans of pop that are half full. It's not pretty and I'm not proud of it, but it is food and when you're this hungry, your stomach doesn't care where it came from.

At times I dream of the meals that Shelley would make for us, the steaming mounds of fluffy mashed potatoes, the golden roast chicken with its dripping juices, and her perfectly spiced gravy. I imagine us sitting around the table, laughing, and the feeling of perfect satiety in my stomach from having both my physical and emotional needs met. The scene is so vivid in my mind that my mouth waters; I can practically taste the food. Then tears prick my eyes as I realize how ashamed Shelley would be of me right now. This is not the life she envisioned for me, this I know.

Chapter 23

I've been a wreck since seeing Jacqueline on the street. It shouldn't have come as a surprise to me to see her there; after all, I was fairly sure that if she were still alive, she'd probably be living the same way. Every social worker I've had has reported the same thing to me about the state of her lifestyle. I used to harbour so much anger towards her. Anger for being a poor caregiver and for hurting me, anger for not being the mother I needed. I would be so angry for what might have been, like if I had just wished hard enough, she'd turn into someone else and welcome me with open arms ready to love me. Now I understand that Jacqueline isn't capable of being what I wanted her to be. And seeing her after all these years, I realize that the anger has mostly melted away. Instead I feel a deep sense of pity for her for all of these years wasted. For a relationship with her daughter wasted. For her life wasted.

I've been crying so much lately, releasing pent up feelings that I hadn't even realized I'd been holding all these years. Austin has been super supportive of me, holding me close and letting me grieve.

I want to talk to Trina, to let her know what's happened, so when she bursts into the apartment first thing in the morning, I run to give her a hug. She smiles, happy to see me, and I feel hopeful about her for the first time in a long time.

"You okay?" I ask her. She hugs me close and smiles again.

"I'm good," she assures me. She kicks off her shoes and heads into the kitchen.

"I'm just going to make breakfast," I tell her. "You want some?"

Trina peers over my shoulder at the frying pan I've got on the stove, the butter forming a puddle. She nods and my heart leaps at the chance to have breakfast with her. I crack a few eggs into the pan and shake salt and pepper on them. Trina watches as I put two slices of bread into the toaster. She takes out two small glasses and the orange juice. I glance over at her arms and see the tell-tale signs of the same compulsion I felt for so many years. She catches my eye and pulls her sleeves down, but it's too late. I've seen the cuts and the scabs. I've seen the damage. I understand the feelings released through each of those cuts. I understand the escape it has given her, and yet it breaks my heart to see the marks mottling her arms. Still, I can barely contain my excitement at her bright smile, how her eyes seem to have light in them again. I work quickly, hoping that I can get us sitting with our breakfast before she changes her mind. I've missed her so much.

We sit face-to-face on the couch, our legs pulled to our chests, our plates resting on our knees. She eats slowly and mindfully, as though she's trying to make it last. I study her face, relieved to see her looking more like herself. After so many weeks of depression and indifference, I want to keep her in this moment. I make small talk before telling her about seeing my mother. She smiles sadly at my story.

"I wonder if I'll ever see mine," she says. "Maybe I should try and track her down." My eyes grow wide with surprise.

"I'll help you if you want," I say, but I'm a bit scared about Trina finding her. No matter how many years go by, the feeling of not being wanted by your mother does not diminish or get easier.

"I've missed you," I say finally. Trina smiles, her gaze fixed on the sky outside our balcony doors. We finish our meals and I scoop up her plate and take our dishes to the kitchen. I quickly wash the dishes and clean the kitchen. It's almost nine o'clock and I have to rush to take the bus to the library to meet with the other participants of the writing program. Our performance is the following week and I want to be ready. Trina is still curled up on the couch and I bid her goodbye before I go. "Want to hang out tonight?" I ask, hoping that we can spend some quality time together.

"Sure," Trina says. "I'd like that." She waves goodbye, still smiling.

"Love you," I call out to her as I head to the doorway.

"Love you too," she replies. I shut the door behind me, my heart leaping with relief that we'll be able to reconnect tonight. My best friend is back.

* * *

When I arrive at the library, Austin waves at me from behind the front counter. I see the long line-up of patrons waiting to get their books signed out, so I wave and continue on to the conference room where our group will be meeting. I'm nervous about reading my work, but I'm also excited. *Shelley would be proud of me for this*, I think. *She would have wanted this for me and so would Mrs. Assaly.* The other participants are taking turns reading aloud, pretending there is an audience before them. I smile at a few of them and take my place in the room to practise as well.

"How'd it go?" Austin asks me when he's off work. It's mid-afternoon already. I've been reading in the library, waiting for him to finish his shift.

"I think I'm ready," I say, but my stomach flutters at the thought.

"I've got some news," Austin says. He looks more nervous than I've ever seen him.

"What's that?" I ask. He's wringing his hands as he sits next to me.

"I was accepted into the Masters program in Regina," he says. "I can start this fall," he continues. I feel my heart flip-flop at the news. Regina is two and a half hours away. Even though he'd always told me his plans, I can't imagine Austin being that far from me. Austin looks nervous but excited. He's gazing at me intently, looking for my support. I smile halfheartedly, trying to be happy for him, but all I can think of is what I stand to lose.

"And I know this might be too soon, but I can't imagine going without you," Austin says. "Andy, would you come with me?"

I breathe a sigh of relief and smile. Surely I can go to school in Regina too? Although I don't quite know how I'm going to make it work or what it means for me, I know that I want to be with him. I throw my arms around him and kiss him.

"Of course I will," I say, and I mean it. I know enough to know when you've got a good thing, you can't let it go. And truthfully, I know I can make it on my own without him, but why would I want to? For a fleeting moment I wonder what will happen to Trina if I go. All I can think of is getting to be with Austin.

We start discussing our plans, talking over each other in excitement. "I'd like to go as soon as I can," Austin says. "I want to find a place before they're all snapped up by the other students." He has decided to keep his grandma's house and rent it out while we're gone. He's not ready to let it go just yet and has dreams of coming back to it to raise his own family. "But who knows where the world will take us?" he says and I agree. Why limit ourselves when other opportunities may present themselves? But the thought of marrying Austin and starting a family in his grandma's house thrills me. We hold hands as we walk out to his car.

"Trina and I are going to hang out tonight," I tell him. He seems as relieved as I am to hear the news. "She looked great today," I continue. "She seemed like her old self."

Austin drives me to pick up a movie and some of Trina's favourite snacks. I'm practically buzzing with excitement when we pull up to the apartment. I can't wait to spend the evening with her and tell her my news. Surely she'll be thrilled for me, thrilled for us. Austin kisses me good-bye and watches until I get into the building before driving away. I race up the stairs two at a time, hoping that Trina is there so we can talk more.

"Trina, are you here?" I call out when I open the door. I feel a pang of disappointment when I'm met with silence. The apartment is dim; the only noise the hum of the refrigerator. I set down the bag of snacks and walk out to the balcony to look outside. Dark clouds are rolling in quickly and I can smell a hint of rain in the air. I think of Trina and me, each snuggling under blankets talking and laughing like when she first moved in, the rain pitter-pattering against the windows. The air is cool against my skin.

I shiver and rub my arms, hoping that Trina will be home soon. I can't wait to reconnect with her like old times. She has felt so lost to me for so long. I think back to this morning and how vibrant she seemed, how there was light in her eyes for the first time in what has felt like forever.

Thinking I'd like to take a hot bath and put some comfier clothes on, I make my way to the bathroom. I open the door and flick on the light. Standing in the doorway of the bathroom, I glance at myself in the bathroom mirror and brush the hair out of my eyes. I turn towards the tub, the thought of sinking down into a tub of hot water is so inviting. But something is horribly, horribly wrong. It takes a moment for my brain to catch up with my eyes as I survey the scene before me.

I stare in shock. How could there be so much blood in one place? It is almost black in some places against the white of the tub, that at first I convince myself I must be mistaken. And then something clicks and I realize I'm not wrong at all. I gaze at the lifeless body before me. Blood-curdling screams ring in my ears, and I realize that they are coming from me. Surely the knife gleaming in the tub isn't real, surely the deep slashes in her wrists aren't there, surely I'll shake her and she'll spring back to life. Surely she can't be gone. And yet as I hold her, wailing her name, I know as surely as anything that she's not coming back.

"Trina," I sob. It isn't long before I hear knocking on the apartment door. The next thing I know, there is a strange man standing in the bathroom, gasping at the sight of me holding my dead best friend, blood seeping through both of our clothes. He looks at my horror-stricken face and runs for the phone. Emergency crews arrive minutes later, but I can tell from the look on their faces that they know before even getting near her that she is gone. They speak to me gently and carefully as they try to pry her out of my arms.

I sit on the cold bathroom floor, staring at the blood that has taken over the room and I wretch violently. I can feel that someone is rubbing my back while a police officer is trying to ask me questions. But I'm in shock. I look over to Trina who is now on the stretcher. Her face is strangely beautiful. The look of pain I'd been seeing there for weeks is gone. She looks at peace.

But peace doesn't come to me. Instead, tortured images of the awkward position of her body, the pool of blood, and the gaping wounds on her wrists cloud my mind, starting me screaming all over again.

Chapter 24

September 2004

It is September when I am caught. It is my own fault they found me. It is the weekend of the fireworks festival, which takes place at River Landing, a couple kilometres from where I've been sleeping. There are several reasons why I've decided to venture out to the festival. First of all, there will be thousands of people, which translates into thousands of opportunities for me to obtain food. And second, I've loved fireworks from the first time I saw them, when Shelley and Luke took me to the big hill at Diefenbaker Park to see them one Canada Day. I'm feeling lonely for them, and I think seeing the fireworks might make me feel closer to them again.

All I think of is how I'll be able to fly under the radar by blending into the crowds. Darkness is slowly setting in. I'm tired and weary from walking. It's not that it's really been that far but more because I'm not feeling very strong and healthy. I weave my way through the crowd, keeping my eyes peeled for people I might know or for police who are in heavy attendance. I'm hoping for a good view nonetheless, so I make my way closer to the bridge where the fireworks will be set off. Thinking that I should be pretty inconspicuous alongside a group of teens my age, I slide in next to them on the side of the riverbank. They glance over at me and a couple of them snicker.

"Ew," one comments, waving her hand in front of her face. I look down at myself, thinking that I shouldn't be that dirty, but the girls scoot further away from me. I feel my face get hot with shame while they shoot dirty looks at me.

"Miss," someone says, tapping me on the shoulder. "I think you better come with me." It's a police officer standing over me. My mind races to come up with a story, any story that might make me invisible again.

"I'm sorry, you must have the wrong person," I say, playing dumb.

"Bernice Burton?" the officer says. I shake my head no, but it's clear that she's not about to walk away. People around us are staring, the girls to the left of me are watching, wide-eyed. I contemplate getting up and running but I can see from the tight crowds and the number of police officers here that I won't get far. "Honey," she says softly, kneeling down to my level. "It's really best that you come with us." Two other officers have now joined her and I realize that I don't really have a choice after all. I stand up and they lead me up the riverbank with their hands on my shoulders as though they can sense my urge to run.

I want to vomit with fear and hunger and regret at being caught. Where will I go? What will happen to me? Do I have to go back to the Puhlers'? Just how much trouble am I in? But the police officer keeps looking at me with a concerned smile and it's clear she's not here to punish me. She's on the radio talking in codes I can't understand while the other two guide me to the car. They open the door for me and I slide into the back seat. We pull away from the riverbank just as the first firework hits the sky. I listen to the popping sounds as they erupt, scattering brilliant colours across the sky. It's funny how the world as we know it can just change in a flash.

"What's your name, honey?" the police officer says. Apparently she's been asking me several times, but I've been staring out at the sky. I think of telling her what I'm sure she already knows, after all, she's said it already but I can't bear to return to any semblance of my old life.

"I'm Andy," I whisper. She nods and continues driving.

She assures me that I'll be alright. But she is clean and beautiful and has a large diamond ring on her finger. She has authority and a decent paycheque. How can she know anything about how I feel? About the kind of life I've had? She couldn't possibly know the depths of my fear and disappointment at being found, of having to be accounted for. After what feels like hours of questioning at the station and several phone calls, I am fed a meal and then she tells me we're off to take me to the place I'll call home. My knees knock together as we drive. The streets are relatively quiet being that it's the middle of the night.

We pull up to a big old manor that looks like a castle. It's like nothing I've seen before. I look at the police officer, puzzled.

"This is Haywood House," she says. "They're waiting for you."

Chapter 25

It's late at night when I finally make it to the familiar old building. The landscaping is as beautiful as ever and it reminds me of the feeling of wonder I had coming here for the first time on that late night so many years before. Coming back has made me realize just how much I've missed seeing so many of the people here. We are "throwaway girls," kids that are too old to be cute and cuddled, too set in our ways, and too old to be saved because the damage has already been done. But to each other, we're sponges, soaking up every bit of love and praise we can find. We're warriors of our pasts, searching for the part of ourselves that wants to grow into something more than we've been told we'll ever be. We long to be accepted and loved so we create the only family we've got.

I ring the buzzer on the front of the building. I can barely see through my tears. I imagine that Betty will swing open the door to greet me, but then with a sinking feeling, I remember that Betty doesn't work here anymore. I buzz again, becoming frantic, needing to see a familiar face. When the door opens, it's Phyllis. She gasps when she sees my swollen face and pulls me in for a hug. "Andy! Come in!" she says. She quickly shuts and locks the door and holds me close. "Honey, what's wrong?" I can't talk. I can't say anything. She leads me down the hall and soon Madge and Gertie appear as well.

They are all so surprised to see me that I cry harder at the sight of their faces. It's been so long. They all crowd around me, asking what has me so upset. I can see the love and concern on their faces and it makes my heart ache with guilt and gratitude. After all, I am also to blame for this awful tragedy. I was her best friend and I didn't do enough. I could have done more to save her.

"She's gone," I manage to get out.

"Who's gone, honey?" Phyllis asks.

"It's Trina," I say. "She's gone." And though the women have no details, they all pull together for a hug. Although they can barely make out my words, they hold me close. I can't stop crying for the loss of my best friend. And then I cry for the losses of every girl in this building, because if there is something we all know, it is loss.

Chapter 26

I step up to the microphone and clear my throat. I am trembling. The thought of reading my writing to a crowd almost makes me seize up completely. I scan the crowd, hoping to see a familiar face. I spot Austin standing to the left of the plastic chairs provided for the attendees. He is leaning against a bookcase, a wide grin on his face. He gives me a thumbs-up sign and motions for me to begin. He looks so happy and proud of me, and my heart dances with joy at the sight of his beautiful self, how he stands so confident and self-assured. Everything about him is endearing.

I picture Shelley and Luke and Mrs. Assaly in the crowd, their faces eager. I imagine Shelley blowing me a kiss, making sure the others know that she's my mother and that I'm her pride and joy. I even picture Trina sitting there, her trademark scowl transforming into a beautiful smile. She is nodding at me, giving me her blessing to go ahead. I tear up thinking about her, knowing that even if I haven't forgiven myself for her death, she puts no blame on me. A hand waves furiously in the opposite corner and catches my eye. I'm delighted to see that it's Gertie from Haywood. She's frantically trying to get my attention to let me know she is here. She pumps her fist in the air when she knows that I've seen her. I don't see anyone else that I know. Everyone is watching me with rapt attention, eager to hear the words I've written. I wipe away the beads of sweat that have formed on my forehead and take a deep breath.

"When I was thirteen, I thought you were every girl's dream. In fact, you were. On the outside, you were everything a girl could want. You were charming and funny, athletic and strong, handsome and well-dressed. You were assertive and capable. Everyone thought you were a star.

I wondered what you saw in me, plain, good natured me. I was smart and studious, scared of everything and I admired your strength. I couldn't believe that you'd picked me from all of the others. How you told me I was beautiful and that you loved me. I felt so strong, so important for once because I was the envy of so many. I would have done anything for you, until you showed me your love.

How could someone so admired be so cruel? Your hands left imprints on both my body and soul, hot reminders that faded into shades of green and blue. You unleashed your anger and set it on me in the private moments we shared. Every girl wanted to be in my place but I couldn't let them. I didn't want them to feel your love too.

When you left me broken from the inside out, I promised myself that I would never let you hurt me again. I was done with all of the suffering, eager to breathe a breath of hope in my life. I wanted to expose all of your secrets, how your perfect image masked the true monster I knew you for. As it turned out, I was the last to know.

My body had had enough at such a young age. My skin was tired from the constant attempts at healing. My heart was even wearier, carrying the burden of a thousand secrets and lies that you and I shared.

Months of having the envy of all the other girls, surely believing that being with you would be magical. I decided that my status would have to suffer in order for me to be free from you. If only I could expose every part of you, strip you from your identity and leave you for all to see.

I know why you chose me. I was eager and willing to be whatever you wanted me to be in order to feel worthy of being by your side. It is all coming to an end now. Your perfect world will come crashing down and I may finally know peace."

The audience claps and smiles at me. I blush and thank the small crowd. I wait behind the curtain that serves as the backdrop for the stage while the others perform. When the presentation is over, I race out to find Austin.

"You did awesome, sweetie!" Austin gushes, wrapping his arms around me for a hug and lifting me off the ground. I giggle and gave him a playful swat to put me down. "Honestly, that was incredible," he continues. I blush and turn my head to see if I can spot Gertie, but I can't see her anywhere. I want to talk with her for a couple of minutes and thank her for taking the time to come and see me.

"Looking for Gertie?" Austin asks, reading my mind. "She had to leave a couple of minutes ago. She said she had an appointment she couldn't be late for." I feel a twinge of disappointment because it would have been nice to see her. "She told me to tell you that she's sorry she couldn't stay to talk and that you were fantastic," Austin finishes.

"Okay," I say, but Austin can see my disappointment. A few of the listeners come up to congratulate me on my reading and how much they enjoyed it. I thank them all, feeling humbled by the praise. It's exhilarating to have strangers commenting on my work and showing appreciation for it.

When most of the listeners have already dispersed or left, the bookstore staff begin dismantling the seating area and folding up the plastic chairs. Austin starts to help them, smiling with pride and stealing looks my way every chance he gets. I watch his long, lean body as he lifts several chairs at once. He is smiling and joking with some of the staff, letting everyone know that his girlfriend is brilliant and that he's never been so lucky. Feelings of love for him rush through me. He has no idea how much I love him, how I'm the one who has never been so lucky. I giggle as I listen to him go on and on.

"Your reading was so powerful," a soft voice says behind me. I turn to see who is talking to me. A pretty, blonde, middle-aged woman stands smiling with a young girl that looks to be about eight years old, who is a splitting image of her. The girl smiles brightly at me and holds out a small notebook and a pen. "Can I get your autograph, please?" she says. Her mother pulls the girl's hand away and shakes her head, a little embarrassed. Someone is asking me for my autograph? *This is too much,* I think. Then the little girl stares up at me with her big eyes and says, "Oh, please would you? My mom always said you were really special."

I look at her, confused, wondering how on earth her mother would know me. I look to the girl's mother for clarification, but she has already stepped forward and is giving me a hug. I pat her back awkwardly until I smell the most wonderful smell. It is a smell I'd never forget, a smell that meant everything to me as a young child. Apples and cinnamon. The smell of comfort and love. Security and safety. It couldn't be.

I step back abruptly to study the woman's face. Her shimmery blonde hair has tinges of white and her face has creases and crow's feet that I don't remember. But she smiles warmly at me and I almost collapse with shock.

"Mrs. Duggleman?" I choke. She nods and pulls me back in for another hug. This time I squeeze her tight. "Is it really you?" I ask. She laughs and nods.

"It sure is, my dear Bernice," she says. Hearing my birth name sends shivers down my spine. It has been years since I've been called that.

"Why are you here?" I stammer.

"We came to listen to your reading," she says.

"How did you find me?" I ask.

She strokes her daughter's forehead affectionately as she speaks. "I saw a poster for readings from promising young writers at the library, and your picture was on it. Although the first name wasn't the same, I knew it was you as soon as I saw it." I shake my head in disbelief. I look down at the gorgeous girl who asked for my autograph.

"Is this your daughter?" I ask. Mrs. Duggleman nods and pulls her daughter towards her.

"Yes, Bernice. This is my daughter Sierra. She is seven years old." She gives me a knowing look, as though she is remembering the secret morning we shared so many years ago. And now here she is with a beautiful daughter of her own.

"How have you been? Are you doing well?" Mrs. Duggleman asks.

Really, how do I answer that? I've lived what feels like many lifetimes since I was put into foster care at the tender age of nine. I nod, telling her that I'm living on my own, going to school and that I've got a great boyfriend whom I love very much.

She seems relieved. "Won't you please come and visit sometime, Bernice?" she says, handing me a card with her address and phone number. "I'd love to talk more."

I take the card and tuck it into my jacket pocket. There it is. My chance to finally go to Mr. and Mrs. Duggleman's house like I'd wished for so many years ago. I'd spent days dreaming that I'd be her child and we would live happily ever after.

I gaze at Sierra who looks so comfortable in her skin, so confident and poised for her age, so normal. And instead of the grief and jealousy I thought I'd feel, I kneel down and tell her, "You are a very lucky girl to have a mommy like yours, Sierra. And I'm so pleased to meet you." I reach for her notebook and write a little message and my signature. She lights up and shows her mother, as excited as if she'd just scored the autograph of a pop star.

I feel tears start to well up. Mrs. Duggleman and I both stand awkwardly, unsure of what else to say at this moment in the bookstore while staff members mill around. "I've never forgotten you or stopped thinking about you," Mrs. Duggleman says finally. I nod, barely able to maintain my composure. "Please do think of coming to see us." She smiles and wraps me in another hug, the smell of her sending fireworks off in my mind and body as its power transports me back to another time. "You were always amazing, Bernice. I always wanted the best for you," she whispers, bidding me good-bye. I stand stunned, watching as the two of them head for the exit.

Feelings of all kinds are fighting for space inside me. Gratitude. Joy. Longing. Sadness. Curiosity. Mrs. Duggleman was the catalyst that changed my life forever. What would've happened if she hadn't done what she had? Where would I be now? Who would I have become? I have no answers, just questions that keep coming, occupying my mind.

I stand in the same spot for a long time, reflecting. The bookstore has long since cleared out and the staff is preparing to close. The lights are being dimmed and the money in the cash register is being counted.

"You ready, my love?" Austin says in a playful voice and I laugh. He places his hand gently on my back to guide me to the door. I love the way he touches me, how gentle and protective he is. He brushes the hair back from my face as we walk. But I don't think of Marcus and the memories of him touching me that way, or of how he stole the last of my innocence.

Instead I think of Shelley and how she'd stroke my forehead before bed. I think of love and security and the healing of a mother's love and how good memories have the power to outweigh the bad if we let them.

Austin opens the car door for me and watches to make sure that I get in alright. He skips excitedly to the driver's side of the car just to make me laugh. He gets into the seat, buckles his seatbelt and looks at me, his eyes twinkling and so full of love that I feel it to the depths of my soul.

"I love you," he says before backing out of the parking space. I smile as I watch him, his jaw locked and serious as he concentrates on the road. "We're off," he says. "Just me and my girl."

We speed down the highway on the way to our new town, the sprawl of the city getting smaller in the distance. I throw my head back and close my eyes. My mind goes back to Trina and the night she planned to leave Haywood with her boyfriend. How I'd imagined how happy they'd be driving off to start their new life together. I think of her and how happy she'd be for me in this moment.

Then I start giggling uncontrollably, in between kisses from my boyfriend who is driving with one hand, his other wrapped around me protectively. The car is packed with our belongings, my hand resting comfortably on his thigh as we drive, feeling carefree and hopeful. I can't help but realize my good fortune. This time, I'm not imagining it at all.

Acknowledgements

I t turns out that it also takes a village to raise a book.

Special thanks to my agent, Arnold Gosewich, for taking a chance on me. I'd also like to thank the team at Dundurn Press for deciding that there was a place for this book.

To Fawn Nielsen, Maria Deutscher, and Leandra Clarke, who were so generous with their time in providing feedback on the book and support along the way.

To Susan McMillan, you are an absolute treasure and the epitome of an amazing teacher. I am indebted to you for your advice and insight with this book, but more importantly, your friendship.

To all social workers, foster parents, and other individuals who devote their lives to keeping vulnerable children safe.

To all teachers who aim to make a difference in a child's life. Your words have a tremendous impact, and for that I offer special thanks to Denis Sanche and Clement Bertoncini, two teachers whose encouraging words and messages during my early years have always stayed with me. Thank you for teaching that little girl to believe in her dreams of being a writer.

To my mom, for taking the time to read every single draft; you really powered through this book with me.

To my dad, for trying to decipher every excited, incoherent phone call of this journey and for sharing in my joy. You always believed that it was just a matter of time. I wish you could have been here to see the final product.

To Rick, for being an example to me on how to live in the moment.

To my children and to Ben — this journey would be nothing without you.

More YA fiction from Dundurn

Picturing Alyssa
Alison Lohans

Who is the girl staring out of the old photograph? Every time Alyssa Dixon looks at it, even by accident, she finds herself on an Iowa farm in 1931. The past is nothing like Alyssa's unhappy life, her mother severely depressed after the stillbirth of Alyssa's baby sister; escalating bullying by Brooklynne, a popular girl; and a teacher who is unsympathetic toward Alyssa's family's pacifist beliefs.

Why can't Alyssa live in the past with her new friend, Deborah? Yet Alyssa is always pulled back to the present, where things only get worse. Maybe the farm isn't so idyllic, though. Deborah's mother is ill with a difficult pregnancy, and there's so much work. A series of old family photos shows Alyssa unsettling things about Deborah's family, things Deborah seems not to know. Can Alyssa help the baby be born safely, and at the same time work through the overwhelming problems at home?

Beautiful Goodbye
Nancy Runstedler

Maggie's life has been anything but easy lately. So when her best friend Gillian discovers a Ouija board in the attic, it's a welcome relief. While they'd rather be at the mall than babysitting Maggie's brother Cole, the girls figure it will be a fun way to spend a Saturday — asking questions about boys and other teenage dilemmas. After all, it's just a game. Or is it?

Thinking nothing could possibly go wrong, the kids dive in, eager to test the new game, but discover the board will change their lives in ways they couldn't have imagined. The trio ends up with more than they bargained for and are thrust into a whirlwind journey. One from which they might never return, if they aren't careful.

Chasing the White Witch
Marina Cohen

Teased by her older brother, bullied by the popular girls at school, and plagued by a blistering pimple that has surfaced on the tip of her nose, twelve-year-old Claire Murphy wishes she could shrivel up and die or spontaneously combust. But when a mysterious book appears at her feet in the checkout aisle of a grocery store, Claire is confident all her troubles are over. Following the instructions carefully, Claire dives nose-first into reeking remedies, rollicking rituals, and silly spells. It's only when she recklessly disregards the Law of Three that the line between good and evil blurs and Claire must race against time to undo all of the trouble she's caused.

The Baby Experiment
Anne Dublin

Johanna is a 14-year-old Jewish girl who lives in Hamburg, Germany, in the early 18th century. She feels stifled by the daily drudgery of her life and dreams of seeing what lies outside the confines of the Jewish quarter. Johanna lies about her identity and gets a job as a caregiver at an orphanage. Until it's too late, she doesn't realize a secret experiment is taking place that results in the deaths of babies.

Deciding to kidnap one of the orphans, Johanna sets off for Amsterdam. She faces many dangers on her journey, including plague, bandits, storms and, not least of all, anti-Semitism. Johanna has a lot of courage and determination, but will it be enough to save the baby and reach her destination? Will she finally find a place where she can be free?

DUNDURN

Visit us at
Dundurn.com
@dundurnpress
Facebook.com/dundurnpress
Pinterest.com/dundurnpress

MIX
Paper from
responsible sources
FSC® C004071